# Degree In Irony

Dennis F. Hagan

iUniverse, Inc.
New York  Bloomington

**Degree in Irony**

*iUniverse books may be ordered through booksellers or by contacting:*

*iUniverse*
*1663 Liberty Drive*
*Bloomington, IN 47403*
*www.iuniverse.com*
*1-800-Authors (1-800-288-4677)*

*Because of the dynamic nature of the Internet, any Web addresses or links contained in this book may have changed since publication and may no longer be valid. The views expressed in this work are solely those of the author and do not necessarily reflect the views of the publisher, and the publisher hereby disclaims any responsibility for them.*

*ISBN: 978-1-4502-1994-5 (sc)*
*ISBN: 978-1-4502-1993-8 (ebook)*

*Printed in the United States of America*

*iUniverse rev. date: 03/24/2010*

This Novel Is Dedicated To The Life & Memory Of Frank Moore: A Good Man Who Stood For Family, Principle & Education.

# Chapter 1:

The venture home from work today took a little longer than usual. There is something about wet road conditions that compels inadequate automobile owners to jam on their brakes, clogging up highways and intersections. Such events inspire road rage and traffic violations.

Like always I remove my tie the instant that I am comfortably sitting in my Saturn sedan. The colorful collection in the back seat allows me to have a sufficient choice of neckwear when I am running late in the morning.

Before I run through the rain to our two bedroom apartment I must remember to get the days mail. I fool around with my keys before finding the correct one to open the miniature sized mail box that is clustered among 14 others along the entrance of the apartment complex. At first glance all I see are bills.

I quickly shut the slot, remove my keys and head towards home. As I march towards my door, the wet keys slip out of my hands and onto the concrete walkway. "Perfect," I mutter aloud. I quickly grab the keys and make it to my door. Finally out of the rain.

Before I can rest the mail on the counter my cell phone begins to vibrate. Before checking the phone I already know who it is.

I look at the screen, take a deep breath, and answer "Hi Mom."

"Are you home yet?" She replies "It's ugly out there!"

"Yeah I just got home. Your baby boy is safe." I said.

"You know I love you more than anything." She answered back.

"I love you too Mom."

"What are you making for Dinner?" She asked.

"I don't know yet. I'm gonna sit down and relax for a minute." I said as I wondered to myself what was on TV tonight.

"Okay well I'll let you go then. Talk to you tomorrow." She said.

"Alright Mom Good bye" I said before hanging up the phone.

Normally I would let the mail wait but something on the bottom of the stack caught my attention. It was an unmarked envelop with a Florida address. I didn't know anyone from Florida, did I? I open the letter and scan its contents. It is an invitation for a memorial dinner downtown in remembrance of local men and women who lost their lives in the war in Iraq and Afghanistan. I lay down the invitation and begin to think about 9-11 and how I almost enlisted into the army and how my mother convinced me not too.

To get my mind of the somber recount I flip through the remaining envelops. Another envelope stands outs. The senders name is familiar one I haven't seen in many years. I tear open the envelope to see inside is another invitation. This time the event is for my ten year high school reunion. "Wow" I thought. Has it already been ten years? I hold both invitations and sit down on the couch.

# Chapter 2:

"You are the youth, you are our future. It is you and your peer's responsibility to uphold the standards in which you have been taught to ensure a promising tomorrow."

These were the words of our school's guidance counselor. It sounded like she was reading a script. It could have been written on a bumper sticker. These words were spoken to me during my freshman year, before I was suspended for fighting. It's not like I started the fight or anything, I was only defending myself from an older student, and still I was lectured about making the right decisions. I was more worried about how Dad was going to react to the news. I didn't care that the school was giving me a pink slip and a three day vacation, but Dad had enough the hassles with work, and the last thing he needed was grief about his son.

As I sat there in this plastic orange chair that was manufactured before the school opened its doors in the 50's, being reprimanded by a woman who tripled my age, I thought to myself how the hell she can think that she relates to me or any other student at school. She wore this outfit that was outdated in the 1980's; spoke with a dialect that appeared to be of old English and her hair smelled of moth balls. Okay so maybe I am exaggerating just a little bit, but how can students at that age connect with a guidance counselor who was raised in a generation where one was considered to be lucky if their parents had enough money to afford a 13" black and white television set that would be proudly positioned in their living room as I spent the majority of my teenage years "surfing" the internet. I think it's safe to say there's not much of a comparison.

Looking back I now understand what this woman was saying to me, but at the time I thought how can one individual impact society? I am one person, one grain of sand buried among millions. I thought this was something that adults said to children to keep them in line. While the "times" have changed, and innovations and new social environments have dramatically reshaped the playing field, it is common experiences and gained wisdom that link the generations.

Not often enough do we appreciate the advice that has been given to us. Too frequently do we endure a hard life's lesson in order to learn from our mistakes? It was never my intention to go back and change anything I had done. Life is filled with regret and we are not handed many second chances. Knowing what I know now I don't think that I would want to change anything, maybe because I don't think I would know how.

My father always said that there was a reason why they put erasers on pencils. Sometimes you just need to stay away from those ball-point pens.

# Chapter 3:

I grew up in a big city and I loved it. It's what I was used too. Anything other than the hustle and bustle of the city life seemed monotonous as our neighborhood was flooded with kids my age and there was always something to do. The opportunity to get into trouble presented itself quite too often.

As a child it was hard to envision my Dad in his youth. He was more like a dictator than a father. I hear his voice in my head saying "This isn't a democracy," when his authority was questioned. "No" was the answer we had grown accustomed too, and we rarely ever heard its counterpart few and far between. My mother on the other hand was much more accommodating. You could even say she babied us, it's what mother do I guess.

As a joke, Dad would say "There is no laughing in this household!" He had his own sense of humor, if you could call it a sense of humor at all. After lecturing my older sister, younger brother and me, he would always finish with "you'll understand when you're older."

We grew up in an Irish Catholic section of the city, although my parents had decided to send us to public school. My father was raised catholic, but did not particularly feel that he benefited from the structure and ideals instilled from the archdiocese. "I don't have to be in church for God to hear my prayers," I once heard him argue to his mother. I know it's never a good idea to discuss religion and politics in public but everyone is entitled to their own opinion.

However, it is often criticized that a "public school education" is insufficient. Critics say it lacks the values and discipline that a catholic, private or a charter school deem necessary to shape the minds of the youth.

Educators across the spectrum, however, are finding that it is becoming quite a difficult task to educate those who do not have the intention of learning. How can success be derived from a room full of failures?

John Adams High School attempted to separate its students into different levels of learning, in hopes of providing an adequate learning environment for its more gifted students. And what pray tell do you ask would happen to the remainder of the student body? Just hope they have a few teachers who intend to make a difference in the class room rather than counting down the days till retirement.

School has been and will always be a heightened social environment; where one needs just a little more that book smarts to survive, or maybe it was just like that at my high school.

When my senior year finally arrived, it would be a year to remember. John Adams High School was home to the Adams Explorers, over 3,500 students and 220 plus staff and faculty members. From the outside it looked like a prison, from the inside it was run like anything but. John Adams was the first institution of learning in the city to "boast" the use of metal detectors and scanning identification cards, a nice sense of security provided by the city school board.

Adams was home to a wide array of races and ethnicities. There was an article in the Daily News where teachers proudly stated "our students embrace the multicultural environment." One reporter coined Adams the melting pot of the city. The majority number of students was white, the percent roughly falling around 46%. Black students made up about 33 % of the student body, and rounding off the remaining classmates were the Asian, Indian, Russian and Latino persuasions. To most of the students, skin color really didn't matter; we were accustomed to this sort of diversity since grade school.

Every school has their stereotypical student groups and John Adams High School was no different. Since this school was *praised* for its multicultural learning environment the students were somewhat used to it.

As a student at John Adams, you soon fell into a routine, trying hard to not fade into the shadows while also avoiding social scrutiny as you passed through the flooded hallways. Students knew their respective roles, even in high school there is a social hierarchy that dictates how you should dress, talk and act. Most of the faces roamed the hallways were familiar.

As a freshman you wait your turn, you climb the ladder to "Seniority" and you come to find out you have run out of rings. We reached the top, the persistence has paid off, and the moment last shorter than expected.

I did not realize it at the time, but certain events that would follow would greatly impact my life, all it takes is a few small ripples to redirect the tides.

# Chapter 4:

*September 7*[th] *1997*

It was my first assembly in John Adams High School. Our home room advisors escorted us into the auditorium and were it a sight to see. Just about the entire room was filled with 1st year students. Noise echoed from wall to ceiling, a surreal sense of organized chaos lingered throughout the auditorium. The large assembly hall could seat around 3,000. This room was used for assemblies, concerts, plays and other organized lectures and such. The auditorium was set up in three sections, with four aisles leading from the entrance down the raised stage. A large center aisle split the three sections in half so that it was easier for a packed congregation to exit through the 7 exits. The large stage was raised about four feet off of the ground was complimented by the massive navy blue curtains the hid the back areas of the stage. A tiny podium sat center, as the stage appeared all but empty.

An unfamiliar looking man slowly walked to the podium. He was a rather tall slender man, with thinning black hair and an appropriately matched mustache. He looked like your normal teacher. If you looked at his forearm he would have a school board stamp of approval on it.

"Can I have your attention, can I have your attention please!?!" His deep voice roared through the speakers.

He waited a few seconds before he continued. "Welcome to John Adams High School, I am your principal. My name is Dr. Harry Cald." Principal Cald clears his throat, and then pauses again to allow the remaining students to be seated and surrender their undivided attention.

"You are no longer children. *(Clears throat)* You are now young adults and you will be treated like adults. This is not elementary school, there is no recess or nap times offered at John Adams High School, play time is over. This is your last destination until you reach the real world. *(Coughs)* The decisions you make from this point forward will ultimately dictate your path in life. *(Clears throat and pauses)* You are now responsible for your actions, not your friends, not your parents, not your teachers, and certainly not me. *(Coughs)* Your teachers and I will all be here for guidance and support. This is your lives people and the future is now. *(Clears throat and pauses)* Do not get lost in the past or present. Take a look to the person to the right and left of you. On your graduation day one of these people will not be sitting with you. Do not let it be you. *(Coughs)* Welcome to John Adams. Please enjoy your time here; I encourage you to make the best of this situation and reap all of its advantages. *(Clears throat)* We want you to succeed not only in the classroom, but outside of it as well.

Theodore Roosevelt once said that "To educate a man in mind and not in morals is to educate a menace to society."

"Thank you and enjoy the rest of your day."

Principal Cald had proceeded to walk off the stage. The large auditorium that was once filled with laughter was silenced by Principal Cald's welcoming to High School. You could have dropped a pin. There's nothing better than brutal honesty to get young men and women motivated. These words would strike a chord with many of these students as it enraged some and it inspired others to succeed, life is all about perspective.

A student by the name of Bobby Jackson was greatly offended by Principal Cald's statements. Before Principal Cald could exit the auditorium Bobby let him know how he felt about his speech.

"Fuck you man, I'm gonna graduate. Ain't nobody telling me that I'm not graduating." He screamed.

Bobby then grabbed his bag and stormed out of the auditorium. Not one teacher made an effort to stop Bobby. No discipline was given to the disgruntled student, we all just watched him leave unattended too. The door had slammed behind him and nervous laughter filled the room. Teachers began to instruct students to exit and proceed to their first period classes. I thought that this was quite an introduction.

On this day there were just fewer than 1100 students that sat in the auditorium. We were all scheduled to graduate in the spring of 2001.

### *September 12<sup>th</sup> 2000*

It was the third day of senior year and we were on our way to our first senior assembly. The exhilaration of being the alpha males was still fresh in our systems. The auditorium was alive, full of laughter and excitement. Over 11 years of education had accumulated until now. All the homework, pop-quizzes, term papers, projects and tests added up to this moment. This is the year where "Senioritis" kicks in. We can see the light at the end of the tunnel. Many had imagined they would coast through classes all the way to graduation day. Teachers know this is our last year, they'll just cut us some slack and we were planning on taking full advantage.

In the midst of making weekend plans Principal Cald, like always, slowly walked to the podium center stage:

"Congratulations ladies and gentlemen, you are now seniors, and you have accomplished absolutely nothing! *(Clears throat)* Do not think that because you are 10 months away from graduation day that this will be a cake walk for you, it surely will be anything but. *(Coughs, pauses for a moment)* If you would take a look around the room you will see that there is a significant difference in the number of student then when you were here for the first time as freshmen. *(Clears throat)* If you recall the first time I had spoken to you I had informed you this would happen. There were 1084 students sitting in front me that day, today 678 sit here before me and still some of you will not be sitting here in June." *(Coughs)*

Some of us who remembered the outburst glanced over at Bobby Jackson, who was now smiling. There were rumors going around that he had already landed a scholarship to play football at the University of Maryland, even though he had yet to play a single snap his senior season.

"Some of you will continue your education at the collegiate level; *(clears throat, pauses)* others will enter the real world at the year's end. This will be one of the most important years of your life, it is imperative that you act accordingly.*(coughs)* While you have come a long way from your freshmen year, strides are still left to be made. Your journey lies ahead of you and it will truly start at the year's end. I advise you to be prepared. *(Coughs)* As always your teachers and I will be here for any advice and guidance that we can provide. *(Clears throat)* Good Luck! You are going to need it. "Principal Cald stepped away from the podium and walked off stage. Principal Cald had a special way of killing the mood.

At a parent-teacher conference Principal Cald was asked why he spoke with such an insensitive tone to his students. His response was simple and just. He believed that students needed a wakeup call. He told concerned parents that "Generation after generation walks through these halls with a shorter grip on reality. It seems to me that parents have become accustomed to sheltering their children from the real world. So much so that they have presented their children with a false sense of reality and unfortunately it will eventually come back to haunt them. I understand that as a parent you want to protect your child but you cannot protect them forever. As an educator and positive role model in my student's lives it is my job and responsibility to be completely unbiased and to assertively prepare my students for the rough road that begins after high school. I would love to tell them that they are all going to be successful and that life is going to be easy for them. Unfortunately it just doesn't work that way; if I did not make an attempt to be direct and honest with them than I would fail to do my job."

You really can't blame the guy on his logic. Looking back I can now I agree with what he said. As Americans, we can live very sheltered lives. The freedoms and privileges that we have are sometimes overlooked and taken for granted. Many of us do not fall victim to the horrors that plague no-so-fortunate nations. Parents tend to hide the ugly aspects of life from the ones they love and their perception of the world is not parallel with reality.

We worship media gods that tell us to wish for champagne wishes and caviar dreams. We are to believe that we can achieve our aspirations based on wanting them and not by working for them. Television has created an allegiance of those who believe the world is built on desire and not by merit. This is not the American Dream those before us have laid out. Hard work results in achieved dreams.

How can children prepare for the real world when everything they learn on TV is make-believe? I can understand the idea that parents want to protect the innocence of a child, but a time comes a time to inform them about the world around them. An adolescent mind will one day embark on exploration; it's a good idea to invest in a reliable compass.

# Chapter 5:

The High School Social environment can be detrimental to the self esteem and confidence of many students. Less fortunate individuals can be the subject of constant ridicule and torment during the course of their time in educational institutions. Nicknames will stick, and embarrassing exploitations are rarely forgotten. Word of wise is to tread carefully.

In many cases, bullying itself is the product of an individual's insecurities and the projecting of self deprecation onto those less willing or able to defend themselves.

Growing up I had a minor speech impediment where I had difficulty pronouncing words that included the combination of "ST." After being sent to a "speech therapist," if you can call her that, in elementary school, she had diagnosed that the condition really wasn't that bad and that eventually I would grow out of it. Her cure was simply using the proven method of trial by error. "Pronunciation was inevitable" she told my parents, reassuring them that the condition was minor and there shouldn't be a cause for concern. What she had forgot to mention was she was over loaded with students who needed significant attention and my minor impediment would only increase her already large workload.

As child, having Dumbo like ears didn't help much either. My mother would say that my face would grow into them, and eventually they would, just not as soon as I would have liked.

The summer entering my freshman year of high school I had grown 6 ½ inches. I grew so fast my hips had nearly dislocated from their sockets, I had developed stretch marks on my shoulders and inner thighs. It is quite interesting to wake up one morning and not be able to fit into of your clothes. The occurrence was a blessing in disguise; you should have seen the clothes my mom used buy for me before I was involved in the decision making process, it's no wonder I was teased.

Upon entering High School I had finished well in the placement tests and ranked high in the state percentiles for Math, English and Science. Due to the stellar test scores, I was placed into the advanced learning program at John Adams. The "ALP" was comprised of three sections of students. "ALP" classes were strategically placed in the nicer portions of the school, the majority of which took place in the annex, a separate part of the building. It was the only part of the building that offered air conditioning to faculty and students. Lesson learned: it pays to be smart.

The majority of classmates in the "ALP" program were what you would call bookworms, nerds and dorks; you know future doctors, lawyers and scientists. It's not that I ever had a problem with these gifted students; it was just that some of them felt that my friends and I did not quite fit into the "ALP" mold. Oxymorons indicate that a jock cannot be smart nor can the cruel be kind. No matter what your appearance there is always a correlating stereotype.

To keep things in balance I would retaliate by openly criticizing them on a number of criteria which my friends and I found amusing. There is a certain sense of peer pressure to fulfill. You can't ever lose face in front of your friends. One who is fretful of their public image will always display false representation.

Like many young adults I was concerned with being popular, always aware of what others thought. This started to change the day I met Frank McAdams.

Frank was around 6 foot tall and had a medium build. He had long lanky arms with Chinese symbol lettering tattooed on both biceps. The lettering on his right arm stood for *persistence* while the lettering on his left arm stood for *chaos*. Frank spoke as if he were born and raised in New York. I sometimes think he changed the way he talked just to sound different from everyone else but that was Frank. He always had his jet black hair spiked with a massive amount of hair gel and had matching silver hoop earrings in his ears. Frank also had clear blue eyes and was often called Sinatra or Blue.

Frank was a transfer student from Archbishop Donovan Catholic High School for boys. He technically wasn't a legitimate transfer student in the sense that he one day decided to change schools. You could say that his hand was forced. He wasn't "let go" or expelled from Archbishop Donovan for any particular reason but instead for a rap sheet of minor offenses.

My favorite stories of his include: the time where he initiated a food fight in the cafeteria using condoms filled with ketchup and mustard.

Another time he claimed innocence in a spitball fight, but a nun who was the eye witness to the event "had it in for him." He was charged for starting the ruckus and for his punishment Frank would spend the weekend making 10,000 spitballs and they would have to be presented first thing Monday morning. Frank's father called the school to complain about the ludicrous punishment, and the number was increased to 15,000.

On that fateful Monday morning Frank arrived with two large trash bags filled for his penance and presented them to Sister Mary.

"Francis" she said. "I hope you have learned your lesson, and I hope that there are 15,000 spitballs in those bags."

"Yes, there is, SISTER MARY." Frank sarcastically answered.

"And are you sure about that Francis, it's not like you have a proven track record of honesty?" The nun asked, questioning Frank's integrity.

Using wit and showing blatant disregard for her punishment, Frank dumped the trash bags onto Sister Mary's desk and contemptuously said "Count 'Em!"

Last but not least, a few weeks after the spitball incident Frank had decided to embarrass Sister Mary in classroom for all his fellow classmates to enjoy. Sister Mary had the tendency to grab troublemakers by their ties while "disciplining" them. Frank had purchased a clip on tie and repeatedly spoke out of line, setting the trap, in hopes of having Sister Mary react. Just as planned Sister Mary approached Frank as he sat at his desk, held is tie in her hand, she offered Frank a smile before giving the tie a sturdy pull, the force sent Sister Mary flying to the floor. The stunt received many laughs and gave Frank instant fame in the surrounding catholic schools.

As for Frank's punishment, he was to write a thousand word essay on how he was going to change his behavior and why he was sorry for embarrassing Sister Mary. The next day Frank would provide Sister Mary with a piece of loose leave paper with the picture of Abraham Lincoln pasted to the center. When the dumbfounded nun asked him the meaning behind the picture, Frank would calmly respond "A picture is worth a thousand words."

Valedictorians and class clowns alike had to appreciate the demeanor in which he executed his infamous classroom shenanigans with such an analytical approach. When he originally told these stories to me I called him a liar, but after I got to know him better I realized he was telling the truth, besides who could make up stories like that? When asked why he never attempted such bold exploits in his new home at Adams, Frank said "I've matured."

Frank's father owned a number of car detailing and auto body shops in the tri-state area. Needless to say, Frank knew that he would one day take over the reins of his father's business ventures. He was accustomed to getting what he wanted, either by his father's influence or the quick thinking he developed from watching his business savvy dad converse with clients and prospective business partnerships.

Frank and his father moved outside of the city, but somehow maintained their city address in the school's records in order to attend Archbishop Donovan so that Frank could graduate with his friends. Frank would be expelled for being caught smoking on school grounds for the 3rd time. Normally such an offense would not merit expulsion, but it was just an excuse mounted by a legion of nuns and the principal to get the Frank out of their school. He was someone else's problem now

After being expelled from Archbishop Donovan, Frank refused to attend a suburban school because he said he couldn't stand those "rich pricks." He managed to talk his way into John Adams, and would openly criticize the public school for its severe disparity in disciplinary tactics and weak course schedule, we became friends immediately.

Frank had the ability to not care what so ever what anybody thought about him. He also made it a point to insult those who criticized him. He was highly opinionated and unsuspectingly sharp. He said what he meant and he meant what he said. He did not succumb to peer-pressure, yet he was extremely critical of others.

As young men we face an overwhelming sense of pressure from fellow classmates. Many times do we try to hide our personal insecurities and short-comings. A young man faces the demands of alcohol, drugs, sex and breaking rules. If you did not participate in the aforementioned activities the repercussions could be severe and nobody wants a "soft" reputation. If you didn't drink you weren't "cool," if you didn't have sex then you must be "queer." if you adhered to all the rules then you were a "pussy." If any of these adjectives were stapled to your reputation it would be detrimental to your social standings. Such is life.

We live in a society where we are judged by our physical appearance; our looks and weight, by our intelligence, by the money that we have or don't have, by our sex and race. It is only fitting that this sort of judgment begins when we are young and insecure.

Parents and teachers fret upon the influence of peer pressure on a child's decisiveness but somehow turn a blind eye on the power it yields.

If and when I ever used the excuse that "everyone was doing it" to mom she would ask "If everyone jumped off the Golden Gate Bridge, would you do it too?"

I always answered her tedious question with the simple response "Yes!" When is the last time you've heard a bunch of school kids jumping off a bridge to prove a point?

The first week of freshman year, a student by the name of Robert Green was being teased by a few of my classmates and soon to be friends. Skittles were being launched at his head while he sat there and did nothing. I felt bad for Robert, but I laughed at the little prank anyway. I was handed a few skittles of my own to throw. I had the decision to take a stand and disagree with what they were doing and possibly face ridicule of my own, or to fit in and to throw some skittles. I choose the latter.

The school hallways were constantly filled with the tension and the desire to be popular. Self confidence is contagious, some have it, and others want it. Confidence can be difficult to possess when you are always worried about fitting in with the "In Crowd."

I wanted to be able to march to the beat of a different drummer.

# Chapter 6:

For me, the school year did not really start until the basketball season. I was playing the sport since I was seven years old and it had become a dynamic part of life.

Like many boys my age, I watched in awe as Michael Jordan gracefully flied through the air, dazzling fans with electrifying dunks and gravity defying lay-ups. His trademark style and competitive perfection created an entire nation to want to "Be Like Mike."

I begged my parents to buy me Nike sneakers, drank endless bottles of lemon-lime Gatorade, wore Hanes underwear and I even thought of sporting the shaved head look like to pay tribute to his Air-ness, but then I remembered I had huge ears. I collected NBA trading cards and religiously wore a replica #23 jersey I received one year as a Christmas gift. I even wore his self titled line of cologne. I never did dangle my tongue during a lay-up; I probably would have bitten it off.

After being cut from the junior varsity during freshman year try outs I promised myself it wouldn't happen next year. I practiced every day after school, on the weekends and during any other free time I could. When I watched TV I would lie on the couch and meticulously toss the basketball, hoping to perfect my shots rotation.

Being a white player in the city's public league did not come without hostility. It was difficult and extremely intimidating as we traveled across the city and playing in the surrounding neighborhoods. My first junior varsity game could be compared an initiation of sorts. The experience took place in the southwest section of the city at Westmont High School. A few weeks prior to our basketball game there was a riot on the schools premises' that resulted in 15 arrests. Six teachers, thirteen students and two security guards were sent to the hospital after the violent demonstration of student revolt. It was said that it took police officers and school security over forty five minutes to regain order. An estimated 313 students were involved in.

Local media hounded the school, as the press brought about more negative attention to the city's public school system and its inability to maintain safety inside the schools and educating the children. A tarnished image of education had plagued the section of the city for over three decades, and there was no indication that things were about to change.

I was anxious come game day and I was just about petrified when our team arrived at Westmont High School. I can be honest when I say that I never before was afraid for my life until this day. After exiting the bus I kept my head down low and followed the rest of the team and our coach to the locker room. I was looking forward to getting this game over with and having learned from the experience. There could not be a more frenzied environment for scholastic athletics.

I sat on the bench and nervously watched the game. It is rare when an athlete would rather sit out for the games entirety, not be given the chance to compete, but this time I wanted to be a spectator. I was waiting for the final buzzer, so that I could board the bus so I could get the hell out of there.

Around the second quarter I noticed a fan sitting in the stands. He was staring at me for quite some time, it seemed like a good five minutes had gone by before he again blinked. I did my best to not look at him but couldn't help it. For a split second we made eye contact. Quickly I turned my attention back to court but it was too late. He stood up and from across the arena shouted "I'm gonna kill you white boy" as he motioned a cutting movement across his throat.

A teammate we called "Hollywood," who was sitting next to me, looked over to stands and received a similar outburst from the hostile fan. "Turn your head around sellout, you wannabe nigga!" He yelled.

The black players on our team faced another kind of harassment from teams in the rougher parts of the city. Many of the players on our team transferred to John Adams for a better education and a safer learning environment. They had to take two buses to get to school in the morning and then two again at night. Leaving their neighborhoods for a white school was seen as an act of disrespect and they were often reminded about it on the court.

*Dennis F. Hagan*

Our team was losing quite badly and I was playing the majority of the second half. My mind was elsewhere. I was not used to this type of environment. I was visibly shaken and dogs and bees aren't the only living creatures that can smell fear. A few times as I posted up in the lane jockeying for position unsuspecting elbows were thrown to my chest, and just about every time I was back on defense they would taunt **"mismatch, mismatch, I got the white boy."**

The game would end, we would board our bus and we would go home. This experience would be taken with me. It would not be the last time; however, that I would face intense playing conditions.

# Chapter 7:

The first day of varsity tryouts seem like a forgotten memory. Adrenaline was racing through my body. I was excited to get on the court and make a statement. I was going show Coach Williams how much I had improved in the off-season and prove that I deserved a spot in the starting lineup.

I hit the gym hard putting on over 10 pounds of muscle and strength. My father had installed a hoop in the driveway when I was ten years old and all the practicing in the rain and cold was going to pay off. All summer long I practiced dribbling and shooting with my left hand. I would repeatedly throw the ball off the side wall of our house to imitate a catch and shoot. I executed calf raises until my muscles burned. I was ready.

The gym was packed with over 100 varsity hopefuls and there were only 14 roster spots. Many players would go home with broken dreams and I was not going to be one of them. Another returning player looking to secure a starting position was Harvey Sanderson.

Harvey was a point guard who was just under 6 feet tall. He has a smaller build but was stronger than he appeared. Harvey wasn't super quick or electrifying at the point of attack but he was a very good ball handler and a sniper on the court. Harvey and I were playing together for a few years now and we played very well together. We had high expectations for the season and spent the weeks leading up to tryouts practicing together.

Intimidation is a way of life on the hardwood. Players will strategically use mental games to keep their opponent off balance. I rarely engaged in mind tactics unless someone really got under my skin and I lost my nerve. At this point off-color remarks and taunting had no really effect on how I played. For the most part they were effectively blocked out and used as fuel.

Coach Williams would say athletics is 90% mental and 10% physical. Every time you step on the field of battle you need to have the confidence that you are going to dominate anyone in your path. I always wanted to be the best and it was my intention to play as such. When expectations are high anything short of perfection is unacceptable.

As the tryouts progressed I felt more confident in myself and my game. I was proving to others that I was a force to reckon with. Defense is the cornerstone of any balanced players attack and I learned early on that defense wins games; offense fills the stands. It doesn't matter how much you can score, if you can't stop your opponent you will never gain the competitive advantage.

I was given the nickname "garbage man" during junior year try-outs and the name stuck. Coach Williams said I had an ugly shot, because I held the ball high over my head and it looked like I was throwing garbage bags. The name also was attributed because a lot of my scoring in practice came from offensive rebounds and put backs. What you would call garbage points. I didn't mind the name that much. It was better than some other nick names on the team.

# Chapter 8:

Tryouts had come to a conclusion and the team was trimmed down to 14 players. Coach Williams began to prepare us for the season.

"You are going to be well conditioned machines." Coach Williams would yell as he enforced his strict cardio vascular exercises. The first week of practice we didn't touch a ball. His preseason conditioning program had intensified over the prior year. Coach Williams had missed the playoffs four consecutive seasons and he was determined to not make it a fifth.

"If you cannot run and jump in the 4th quarter like you can in the 1st, you will not win the game," he would say as he demanded countless suicides and never ending laps around the gym. When we were not running, Coach Williams commanded sit-ups, push-ups and leg lifts. He felt calisthenics were beneficial to increase strength and stamina. If anyone were to complain about his vigorous conditioning methods Coach Williams would simple say "I'm sure I could find someone who would gladly run wind sprints in your place."

When he finally thought we were ready, we were then allowed to start practicing with the ball.

Coach Williams wasn't the type of guy to pull a punch. He was normally enjoyable to be around and brought a sense of confidence and enthusiasm into our locker room. When disciplining or instructing his players he was quite boisterous and his loud voice echoed with intensity. You definitely did not want to fall onto his bad side. He had a tendency of intimidating his players and a more sensitive athlete could easily be turned off by his tactics. To ease the tensions after an intense practice Coach Williams would often say "Listen to what I say, and not how I say it." He was just as quick to congratulate a player for performing well as he would condemn a player for making an error.

Coach Williams was a former semi pro baseball player, he also played a little college basketball as well. He only stood 5 feet 8 inches but he was athletic and powerful.

During tryouts he kicked a guy out for wearing a collared shirt. Coach Williams said to the student "Hey Tiger Woods, this isn't the golf team. This is Varsity Basketball and when you play basketball for me you wear basketball attire." Coach Williams lived by the motto if you look good, you'll play good.

On a Thursday afternoon before practice, Harvey had approached me with a grin on his face and a newspaper clipping in his hands. "Ah, check this out." Harvey said and he handed me the local paper. Harvey had the tendency to add "Ah" to the beginning or end of each sentence.

The Daily News wrote an article about the public basketball league and how the teams were preparing for the start of the season. The article offered a few short paragraphs about all the school's team and even mentioned seven key players for every team. I read with anticipation and my eyes were drawn to the bold letters that read **John Adams Explorers.** Just as I had hoped I saw my name in the article, misspelled as usual but it was me none the less. Harvey's name was listed right under mine.

"AH, you better get your own copy and cut it out." Harvey said as he took back the paper.

"Oh you know I will." I said with a large smile.

When I got home that day after practice my mother had already cut the out the article so that I could save it. I think my parents were more excited about the article than I was. They saved every clipping I was in for the last few years. It wasn't much to look at yet but I was planning on a big season with a lot better articles to add to the collection.

My father was my biggest fan and toughest critic. I could have a 25 point game and I would be lectured for missing foul shouts or not boxing out hard enough for rebounds. At one point he was my coach and attended every game I played in up until high school.

He was hard on me, as fathers often are. Their intentions are for their sons to be the best, and dad knew that being the best took a lot of hard work and practice. He also felt that it was a waste of time to be sensitive about constructive criticism.

Just about a week before our first game, right after Coach Williams informed me I secured a starting spot. He addressed the team with a highly motivating speech. I wasn't sure if Coach Williams was a religious man but on this particular day he spoke with great conviction.

"I have high expectations for our team this year gentlemen, yes I do. We have the talent and the character to be successful. Oh yes we most certainly do. I know that we have a tough schedule but there is no reason why we should not make the playoffs, no there is not. We are going to turn some heads this season, oh yes we are. We have some guys on this team that can play college ball next year; Tyrone, Jerry, Keith. And I am going to see that you get that opportunity."

I felt honored and surprised to hear my name mentioned from Coach Williams in that light. I'm sure that my face had turned red. It was my dream to play at NCAA Division 1 program such as Duke or Notre Dame but unfortunately I lacked the size for the position I played. But I would still dream about having another growth spurt. It happened to Scottie Pippen and Dennis Rodman.

During my senior year I finally developed the skill that all ball players aspire for: the ability to rise up and dunk. The first time I did it was in a practice. We were throwing up alley oops to each other and I got just enough air under my legs as I caught the ball above the rim and stuffed it home. I received accolades for the accomplishment. A few guys chuckled "Some white guys can jump."

When I told my parents about the feat my mother so carefully pointed out that it might be difficult for me to dunk in a game because the size of my hands. Thanks to genetic make-up I was born with wide palms and short stubby fingers, hands not conducive to palming a basketball.

I mentioned that many NBA stars, such as Shawn Kemp, could not palm a basketball and still was able to dunk. Mom then reminded that I was only 6'2" and had "little hands." Eager to joke about the situation I left the room and obtained a bottle of super glue from my father's utility drawer. I quickly placed the adhesive onto my right hand and then grabbed a hold of my basketball. I walked into the living room as my parents were reading different sections of the newspaper and said "Hey Mom I can palm the ball now." The incident still remains a favorite story at family gatherings and holidays.

I was criticized for not using my size and athleticism on a different playing field such as football or wrestling. On a number of occasions I was approached by the head coach of the varsity football team and was asked to try out for the squad. Although I was flattered by his request the fact is that I never played football and the season would interfere with basketball's preseason and conditioning program. I had no playing experience on the gridiron as my neighborhood did not offer local peewee football when I was young.

My father loved baseball as a child and was a center fielder in a fast pitch soft ball league until his late thirties. He instilled in me a love for cleats, batting gloves and running the baseball diamond. My first plate appearance resulted in a grand slam when I was 8 years old. I used to have the game ball saved on my trophy shelf, but I think it more recently became a dog toy. I was a catcher and lived for the pop of the ball in my mitt and the thrill of throwing base runners who taught they could steal a base on my time. Over time my passion for the game faded and I found practice becoming a chore and games were excruciatingly long. After 10th grade I put down the catcher's mask and set my sights solely on basketball.

My love belonged to the hard wood court with its ten foot rims and the sound of basketball sneakers squeaking on the court leaving rubber marks as a sign of respect. In no other sport could you find the creativity that come with offense and the dedication it took to defend. There is no prettier sound in all of sports then a perfect jump shot results in a swishing sounds The ball touches nothing but the bottom of the net and the shooters know there is nothing more satisfying. On the defensive end I found nothing more rewarding than stuffing an opponent's poor attempt of a shot back in their face. Nothing was more exhilarating than boxing out a larger adversary as you muscled for the rebound or nothing more satisfying then executing an unsuspecting "pick," where its victim blindly runs into the screen and falls to the floor as your teammate was now en route to the rim. Basketball offered many intangibles that other sports could not. It was a team mentality and provided camaraderie whose one goal was to win.

After practice I was approached by Coach Williams, "Keith I want you to know that I was serious about you playing at the collegiate level. I think that you most definitely can play for a Division 2 program and I would like to make sure that you get there. You have the heart and determination son, keep it up and don't let me down."

I never told anyone what he said to me that day after practice; I wanted to these words as motivation and encouragement. I would keep them with me as inspiration on the court. It's a great feeling to achieve personal goals and I wanted to enjoy it. The season was to start within a week and I could not wait. Class served as filler in between practices. I was on autopilot.

# Chapter 9:

It was Monday, the day before the season opener and Coach Williams was running late for practice. He was never late, so it came as a shock to be waiting for him in the gymnasium.

When coach finally arrived he steam rolled through the gymnasium like a freight train. He had an awful look on his face. Someone had ticked his off something fierce. For a moment he did not speak a word. He stood there in the middle of the court looking up at the rafters as he appeared to prepare for what he was about to say.

"I'd like to have your attention gentlemen." He said with a low stern voice.

"For those of you who didn't know, the last three years I have been coaching Roosevelt High School's varsity baseball program."

He paused for a second before he began to speak with increased intensity. "Now, The cities High School Athletic Committee rules state THAT if a teacher at a high school wishes to coach a sport in which the current coach is not a teacher at that school, then the outside individual has to relinquish the position upon such a request. Well unfortunately Roosevelt has a new Phys. Ed teacher who has decided that he would like to coach their baseball program."

Coach pauses for a second as his voice grows louder and angrier.

"Now as luck would have it, Coach O'Brien has decided that he no longer has the desire to be the Baseball Coach here at Adams. I was at what you might call the right place at the right time. It was the perfect situation, for the chips had certainly seemed to fall into place. HOWEVER, the Athletic Director here at Adams, Mr. O'Laughlin, made the decision that I was not going to replace Coach O'Brien. No, he felt that the junior varsity coach Mr. Barbin was a more suitable candidate. He was concerned that coaching two sports may take away from the quality of both programs, and we all know that Baseball is a "higher" priority here. This morning the school announced that Barbin was awarded the job and I could apply for the Junior Varsity position as it was now available."

In his three years as Roosevelt's head coach, Coach Williams had won 2 consecutive championships. In his mind he was the more qualified candidate and he probably was. Coach Williams played semi pro ball and boasted hardware that Coach Barbin did not. The only reason he could think of that he had lost the position was that the decision process of Mr. O'Laughlin was based by a racial stand point. Coach Williams would not even look at Harvey or me. "

"It's just plain old bullshit. I guess the black man can coach on the basketball court but he ain't cut out for the baseball field at this school." Coach Williams roared.

The man who had beaten Coach Williams was Max Barbin. He was the JV coach for the past 6 years and was being groomed by Coach O'Brien. The Athletic director was close friends with O'Brien, which turned out to be a major reason why Barbin was picked. Coach O'Brien was the baseball coach for 18 years. He had won 5 championships and made the playoffs 15 times in his career. Coach O'Brien and Barbin both believe in "Old School" coaching tactics and shared a similar philosophy for how the program should be run.

I truly did not believe race was a factor in the decision making process just unfortunate coincidence. Coach Williams, however, did not feel the same way. Coach Williams had his playing experience and won his championships with Roosevelt but Barbin had O'Brien's support. It was a matter of circumstance.

That rest of practice had a morbid tone as there was a clear sense of tension in the gymnasium. The black players on the team instinctively believed that Coach Williams was the subject of racial discrimination. They didn't say much to me or Harvey for most of the practice. Even though we were teammates with most of these guys for two years and developed friendships, we were still white and they felted wronged. Practice was cut early and Coach Williams would end with "Be prepared for tomorrow Gentlemen."

Finally game day had arrived. I was anxious to see if there were to be any aftermath from the previous day's events. I told myself that it would not affect our team dynamic and everything would blow over. The final bell of the school day rang. I ran to the locker room and quickly got changed for the game. When I got on the court to warm up I saw my dad patiently waiting in the stands. He left work early so he could watch the whole game. He had come to all of my home games and a few road ones as well. He didn't travel too much because some of the locations we played at were a little harsh for a man of his skin color. I talked to him briefly before the game. He shook my hand and said "Play hard out there." I smiled and said "You know it Dad."

Coach Williams had decided to do a slight alteration of the line-up which included sitting Harvey and me on the bench for the majority of the game. I barely played three minutes didn't touch the ball and I don't think I even broke a sweat. It was a tough pill to swallow and I was filled with anger and doubt. I hoped the rest of the season would not mirror the day's actions. I hoped Coach Williams was just blowing off some steam. I was wrong.

My father didn't say a word the whole ride home. What could he say? He was almost as angry as I was. When we got home I told him what had happened regarding the baseball incident and he just shook his head.

The rest of the season would unfold in the same manner in which it started. I started a few games here and there but never really got any substantial playing time during the course of a game. Some of the other players on the team stopped passing me the ball and when I was on the court I felt like a ghost. Six games into the season Harvey quit and practices would become difficult without him there as I almost got into a few fist fights during our three on three scrimmages. I still had some friends left on the team but the element had changed.

One day as we traveled for an away game, Coach Williams asked me why Harvey quit. I told him that "He thought he should be starting games rather than sitting the bench." Harvey had not told me this per say but it's what I wanted to say. I was hoping to knock a little sense into him. Coach Williams Johnson did not have a response to my statement he just shrugged his shoulders and turned around.

I eventually asked my father to stop coming to the games. I didn't want him to witness the embarrassment of his son sitting the bench as now 10th graders were playing ahead of me. Dad refused to honor my request and continued to show.

My mom tried to encourage me to ask Coach Williams why I wasn't playing and what I could do to see more action on the court, even though that I knew the answer had nothing to do with athletic ability or game performances. I just couldn't force myself to ask the question, although, I came close on a few occasions, I never mustered the nerve to ask.

I just told myself that if I played hard at practice, defended well and grabbed every loose ball possible, that I deserved more time on the court and that he had no other choice but to play me. Even during the controversy of race, I had earned the respect from my teammates as I was often said to be the hardest working player on the team. Still, determination would not translate into playing time. I sometimes wonder what Coach Williams would have said if I asked him, I guess I will never know.

In the last home game of the season the mounting frustration had reached a boiling point. A majority of the team's players were forced off the team due to their failure to maintain the school boards required grade point average for student athletes. To fill the roster Coach Williams had invited players from the junior varsity team to take their place. Coach Williams had decided to start younger players in the last few games, including my final home game as a senior. Yet another knife in the back. I could barely hold in my emotions. Midway through the second quarter I was finally put into the game. As soon as I stepped foot on the floor an opposing player began to taunt me. "Mismatch, Mismatch, I got the white boy guarding me, I got the white boy guarding me." He cried to his team mates as I defended him. As he recklessly threw a number of elbows in my direction, one made direct contact with my chest and briefly took the air out of my lungs. Next time down he began to throw elbows again and before he could land another, I retaliated by pushing him hard in the back sending him to the ground.

As he regained his composure the player quickly responded by getting in my face and saying "You better watch yourself white boy." Almost now standing nose to nose, I calmly replied "Bring it black boy."

A referee quickly interceded and sent us in opposite directions. A few plays later I would contest for a rebound and my legs would be taken out from under me. I awkwardly landed on my back and the fall resulted in a loud thud. While I lay in pain I looked up to find my adversary standing over me smiling. A foul was not called nor would Coach Williams argue with the referee to have one called. I would be helped off the court and it would be the last time I wore an Adams jersey. As I sat on bench I ripped the jersey off and threw it onto the floor. I had the option of keeping the jersey for $50 dollars, but I never wanted to look at it again.

The remaining games on our schedule were two road games in rough areas of the city and I really didn't feel like facing further racial harassment if I was just going to be a spectator. Racism ended my high school basketball career.

I never considered myself to be a racist person. If I were I don't think I would have been on the basketball team with all black players and a black coach. I had immensely enjoyed the time I had spent with my teammates over the past three seasons and it was an experience that I will always remember. The struggles I faced during the season would change my point of view on issues such as race and equality and I would never be able to let go what happened. I was subject to racial insults, physical harassment on and off the court all because of the color of my skin.

Basketball was a way life. I breathed, slept and dreamt it for as long as I could remember. Color was never an issue; the game was all that ever mattered.

My parents would often criticize their decision of not sending me to a catholic or private school that offered a more sound education and athletics program. Maybe if I attended anything other than a public school I would have had better opportunities but who's to say.

I can't say that things ever really happen for a reason; that our life's plans have been laid out before us. It had not been my expectation for the season to transpire in the manner it did but maybe some good did come out of it. Out of failure I learned that what we want or expect to happen doesn't always mean that's what's going to happen. All you can do is hope that your hard work eventually pays off.

I sat it my room and looked through the scrapbook of newspaper clippings my parents had saved. I became emotional and started to tear out the pages. I ripped up every single clipping and tossed the remains into the trash. Before completely discarding the book, in my hands I held an 8' by 10' black and white picture that was given to me from a friend who worked in our yearbook office. The picture was taken from one of our home games. In the picture I was jumping to block a jump shot. I stared at the picture for a couple minutes, crumbled it into a ball and shot it into the trash can with the remainder forgotten paper.

# Chapter 10:

April 20th 1999 will forever be a day that lives in the minds who witnessed its horror. It's an event where you remember exactly where you were when you heard the bone-chilling news. I certainly remember where I was. I was in my sophomore year of high school. I was at a buddy's house watching music videos on MTV when the regular programming was interrupted by the tragic events.

A small town in Jefferson county Colorado was the victim of a horrific tragedy. Two students had embarked on a shooting rampage at Columbine high school, leaving 12 students and a teacher dead and injuring 23 others before taking their own cowardly lives. Images from the news reports to this day are still buried in my memory as I can still envision a male student dangling from a window as he struggled for his life.

The incident sent shock waves across the United States, leaving many wondering how and why this massacre could happen. Educational institutions throughout the country began to take strong safety precautions to ensure that similar actions would not be imitated in their hallways. There was also a widespread panic against the morals of the Goth culture and its involvement behind the Columbine shootings. Violent music, movies and video games would come into question by parents and teachers as they felt the graphic material had an extremely negative impact on its young viewers.

Others would ask "Where the hell were their parents?"

Adams High School was the first school in the city to install metal detectors at the main entrance shortly after the Columbine incident. With a diverse population of students, school officials wanted to assure parents that their children would be safe on school grounds. It was a preventive step in stopping any replication of the horrible actions that took place in Colorado.

Despite all this, a small group of students became fixated with the social niche that was growing across the nation, which was appropriately named the "Trench Coat Mafia." Two students at Adams High School were suspended for wearing long black trench coats on school grounds. The two students also openly supported the Columbine shooting and warned there were those who felt similar actions needed to take place at John Adams High School. As a result, disciplinary actions were to be enforced on any individual wearing clothing deemed inappropriate and of a violent nature. Anyone who openly applauded the slayings at Columbine was to be suspended indefinitely.

Rumors began to circle that there was a growing number of Adams students who were gathering on chat rooms on the internet and speaking with other members from communities throughout the country gathering ideas and sharing stories. Many thought it was a fad that would soon wear off, dismissing the situation as teenagers rebelling and wanting to voice their distorted opinions while others feared that the growing popularity would result in copy cat like incidents. I never thought I would be affected by the events which rocked the nation in Littleton Colorado.

# Chapter 11:

A couple weeks passed from the media frenzy and primetime documentaries and things began to settle down. Soon enough the mind will digress to the next big thing. Out of sight out of mind or so they say.

The news, which spread like a bad rumor, sent a chill down my spine when I heard it. It couldn't be true it had to be a joke. Ignoring other's comments I immediately went to the source so that I could see it with my own eyes. This was a situation where hear say was thrown out of the window, I had to see it.

The fateful word lay straight across the hall from the school's main office in the men's restroom. I opened the door and walked to the third stall as instructed. I didn't quite see it at first; I don't know how anyone could miss it. It was as clear as day and as dark as night. There before my eyes laid the ominous message. In large red magic marker someone wrote on the wall "All Jocks Die June 1st." I was rendered numb and like those who are witness to a car crash I could not look away.

A week after the threat had been written the entire school was instructed to follow an evacuation drill in the event a school shooting should occur. All students, teachers and faculty member were to exit the school and immediately proceed to the football field and fill in the bleachers. It didn't make much sense to me. If a shooting were to occur there was no way I was going to blindly follow everyone else to the football field. Chances are the shooter was going to be a student with same information regarding the evacuation procedures. Innocent students would be sitting ducks.

As we sat in the stands Principal Cald gave us a speech instructing students to be cautious and report suspicious activities. I really did not pay much attention to what he was saying. I was more interested in who had written the threat on that bathroom wall. I looked at it every day since I heard of its location and the image began to consume my thoughts. I needed to know who wrote the morbid message. Another week would go by and the message still lay on the wall and I thought to myself, why the red marker was not painted over yet. Teachers urged students to provide any information that could so that school police could discover the identity of the student, but apparently no one knew who did it.

# Chapter 12:

Normally I got to school fairly early and I was usually one of the first students to arrive to our home room period every morning. Routinely I walked into the classroom put down my book bag and jacket if it were could go to the bathroom and get a drink from the water fountain across the hall. I tend to fall into little routines; we grow accustomed to such procedures.

One Monday morning I walked into homeroom and noticed a folded up piece of paper on my desk. At first I thought that it was scrap paper left there from the previous school day. When I got to my desk I saw that my name was written on the paper. I unfolded the letter and here is what it read:

*Dear Keith,*

> *I was born into this*
> *Everything turns to shit*
> *The boy that you loved is the man that you fear*
> *Pray until your number,*
> *Asleep from all your pain,*
> *Your apple has been rotting*
> *Tomorrow's turned up dead*
> *I have it all and I have no choice but to*
> *I'll make everyone pay and you will see*
> *You can kill yourself now*
> *Because you're dead.*
>                         **-Marilyn Manson**

The paper fell from my hands. After first I was shocked, and after the initial moment of fear had subsided I thought the letter to be a joke, one in poor taste, but a joke none the less. Two minutes later my friend Eric walked in to the classroom. Before he could say "hello" I asked him if it were him who left me the letter.

Eric and I had become good friends during high school. He had a unique sense of humor and a contagious laugh. We liked the same music and sports and had a lot of classes together. Eric had dark hair and dark eyes. Many thought he was Italian but Eric was in fact Israeli. Eric also had a strong sense of fashion and normally wore outfits that I wouldn't. He played the guitar and wrote music but he rarely played in front of anyone. We disagreed about many subjects but always had a good laugh with one another.

Eric quickly examined the note his face drew blank and he said "You need to report this to somebody, I think this is serious."

Eric was known to play his practical jokes. I still thought he was pulling my leg. "Come on man, don't mess with me. You did this right? I know you like this kind of music." I said with a sense of nervousness in my voice, as I was still trying to convince myself he was the culprit.

"Look at my face Keith, I am dead serious. I did not write this. You really need to turn that in." Eric uneasily responded.

"Swear to me that you didn't do it." I demanded, as my voice grew louder and more concerned.

"I swear to you on my life. May I burn in hell if I am lying to you!" Eric strongly protested to further plead his case.

I knew that he was telling my truth. I could see it in his eyes as he had a sense of fear in them. Eric was a good friend to me and I would take his advice. I would show the note to our homeroom teacher Dr. Fenstamaker.

Dr Fenstamaker quickly rushed to phone and made a call. A school security officer quickly arrived and escorted me to the school's security headquarters, which was located in the basement of the school.

Officer Gallagher examined the note and asked me a few standard questions:

*"When did you notice the note?"*

*"Is there anyone you know that you think may have done this?"*

*"Why would someone write you this?"*

*"Have you been confrontational with anyone recently?"*

I answered his questions and nothing could be determined from his initial examination. I had no clue as to who would have left me that note. I increasingly began to become annoyed with the situation and asked Officer Gallagher if he could just forget about the situation and let me leave. I was reminded that this was an extremely serious matter and was informed that I could be in danger. I was not permitted to leave until the situation was resolved. I did not want nor particularly feel that I need protection but the officer felt differently.

Officer Gallagher informed me that he was going to go back to the class room and interrogate the students in hope of finding some answers. I was to patiently wait there for further instruction.

Just about 10 minutes later the door had opened, Officer Gallagher had returned. I could not see him as I was now sitting behind a partitioned wall as instructed. He had someone with them.

I felt a rush of adrenaline circulate throughout my body. I was anxious and eager to see who Officer Gallagher apprehended.

"Sit down young man!" I heard the officer say. A moment passed as the unidentified student sat down in the orange plastic chair facing Officer Gallagher's desk "What the hell are you thinking boy? Do realize that you can go to jail for this stunt. Have you not been paying attention to the news with all that has happened the past few months." roared Officer Gallagher. "You don't have anything to say now huh, no catchy little death threat for me?"

A moment of silence passed before the student spoke. Officer Gallagher was a tall, large man with broad shoulders a deep intimidating voice. His breathe smelled of coffee and his clothes of cigarettes. His slicked back black hair shined from the low hanging florescent lights in his otherwise dark office and the demoralizing look he had tattooed on his grizzled was a great indication this man was serious. He was standing behind the now petrified unidentified male student as he continued his interrogation. He made me feel nervous and he was on my side.

"I didn't mean anything by it, it was only a joke" a familiar voice said softly.

"A joke? Threatening someone's life is no god damn joke." Officer Gallagher said as he slammed his hand down on his desk. "Do you see me laughing? Do you?" He asked as Officer Gallagher walked around the desk towards his chair. Officer Gallagher glimpsed out of the only window in the office. A window which had bars on it no less.

"Well I hope you're parents have a better sense of humor than I do because you're going to get the chance to tell them this side splitter when they meet with you at to the District 17 police station." Officer Gallagher bellowed.

"I'm, I'm" The unidentified student stuttered.

"I'm what?" Officer Gallagher snarled

"I'm sorry. It, it was just s-song lyrics." The student said.

"I don't want your apologies, you just keep it quiet until your escort arrives" The officer replied.

I barely could hear his words, but I had recognized his voice. His name was Thomas Garrett. I knew him since freshman year and I couldn't grasp why he had sent me the letter. We were friends or at least we had a few classes together. He let me borrow a few of his CD's before. Sure he may have been a little withdrawn anti-social but I didn't figure him as a kid who would shoot up the school. On no account had I any previous conflict with him. Maybe it was only a joke like he said I thought. I did not want to extend the situation further by making any unnecessary the trip the police station. Instead I decided to take matters into my own hands and confront Thomas right then and there. I stood up and walked around the partitioned wall, and approached the officer and Thomas as they sat at the desk.

"Officer," I said. "I know this guy. We, we are friends. I don't think that he meant any harm."

The large officer quickly jumped up from his steel chair with a look consisting of pure anger. He sternly replied "Son this matter is pretty freaking serious and considering the previous events that have taken place and the fact that I take my job seriously this needs to be handled with…."

I wanted to make my point clear so I interrupted the officer "Excuse me sir, but I do believe that this is something we can resolve just between the three of us."

Officer Gallagher did not receive my interruption with as open arms as I hoped "Sit your ass back down where you were. The proper authorities have been notified along with your parents, they'll get to decide a resolution." Officer Gallagher strongly reiterated.

Shortly thereafter Police Officers arrived to the school. Tom was handcuffed and the officers escorted him to a paddy wagon that was park outside the back of the school. My parents were contacted and were on their way to Adams. There was no getting out of this mess. I wished I just threw the letter out.

We arrived to precinct and my parents remained quite calm during the ride over, much to my surprise. They did not yet see the letter but the police explained its content and its severity. It was not going to be dismissed as a prank. When Thomas's father arrived he loudly asked his son what I had done to upset him enough to write me such a letter. My father's face turned red and my mother did her best to restrain him. "He didn't do a damn thing." My father shouted. My mother reached her hand over and put it on his knee and softly said "That's enough Keith."

After both Tom and I gave our statements to the Officer Riley, Tom's actions were viewed as criminal and I was given the decision whether or not to press charges. I was allowed the chance to discuss the situation over with my parents before I made my decision.

After speaking with my parents I decided that I did not want the incident to go any further and to act like it ever happened.

Before we left Tom and I shook hands and he apologized for his mistake. I accepted his apology and not him not to worry about it.

Tom and I barely talked after that day even though we had English and Science class together for the remainder of the year. I never did understand the letter or what made him leave it for me. A part of me would always be embarrassed that went to the police station and that I almost pressed charges against some who wrote me a death threat and he was half my size.

# Chapter 13:

A few friends and I finished lunch one Thursday morning. I say morning because Adams had so many students there were 5 separate lunch periods throughout the day and that school year I managed to get 2<sup>nd</sup> period lunch which started at 9:50 am. We exited the cafeteria and traveled upstairs to hang out in a familiar spot, the hallway outside of the main offices. We regularly gathered there in the mornings and periodically throughout the day to laugh and joke around before the start of a new class. While others found it more convenient to congregate in more low key areas, we were a little brash and posted up were all could see.

Many of my friends were aides to disciplinarians and school officials. It was an excuse to get out of class so that one could file papers, answer phones and receive special privileges.

We were probably 15 yards away from the Main Office when I initially heard it. It was loud and while it seemed liked it was right behind us it in fact originated from the floor below. The noise resembled a series of mini explosions and could have been compared to a hunter unloading the clip of his rifle.

A sense of panic had set in. Students began to run through the hallways in fear and their frantic screams had replaced the sound of gunshots. The first thing I could think of was the morbid message that was now panted over in the bathroom stall that was less than 50 feet away. A few minutes had passed since the sound of gunfire, a few of us huddled together in the office uncertain as what to do next. A few girls who were crouched over close by began to cry and their mascara ran down their faces. It was a surreal experience despite the recent events that had transpired across the nation and in

John Adams High School. No one ever could have imagined such horror happening at our school. No one ever thinks that something bad is going to happen to them, the mind does not work that way.

As we cowered in fear, praying for our safety, we waited for additional events to unfold. My instincts told me to run for the closest exit but I was with friends and was not in harm. Some students did flee the building and one student used their cell phone to alert the police.

What felt like hours passed were only a few minutes. As we continue to sit there confused and afraid an announcement stormed over the speakers "This is Principal Cald speaking. I would like to ask everyone to please remain calm. There have been no gunshots. I repeat there have been no gunshots. What you heard was minor explosives set off near the cafeteria. The two individuals responsible have been detained by security and have been escorted off of the premises. I repeat again there has been NO GUNSHOTS. The noises that you heard were only firecrackers. No one has been injured and everything is being taken care of. Please go back to your classes and return to your normal schedules. Thank you for your cooperation and patience in this matter, and I apologize for any inconvenience."

Like the letter I received a few days earlier, this was only been a prank. School officials did not take the episode likely. The two male students who set off the fireworks were both arrested and expelled. Security measures were heightened in the school with the hiring of more security officers while patrol cars were stationed around the perimeter of the school.

The fear a school shooting was cemented in the minds of those who witnessed the shortened scare. I did not wake up that day prepared to handle such events and I don't think anyone ever will be prepared to experience a situation such as a Columbine or more recently Virginia Tech University shooting. Fortunately for us our situation did not end in tragedy, but for a brief moment it was real.

# Chapter 14:

It was a Tuesday and I had taken the day off of school, which was no easy task in our household. Getting the okay from my mother to skip a day from school was harder than a death row inmate receiving a presidential pardon; it just didn't happen. I had to be on my death bed to get a day off of academics. Every once in a while you just need to kick up your feet and relax. I had some catching up to do with the old TV. Maybe it was because I was doing well in my classes or the recent student activity at Adams, but I had talked my way into a day off and I was feeling quite proud of myself.

A little after one o'clock I received an unexpected phone call. When I heard the phone ringing I thought it was going to be mom checking up on me. I was wrong. I picked up the phone and heard a hurried "Hello?" It was Eric who had an uneasy tone in his voice "Keith, I can't believe you weren't here for this!"

"Here for what?" I asked. Now growing increasingly curious.

"They found out who wrote on the bathroom wall!" he exclaimed.

The hair on my neck stood still; I could not speak a word as syllables proved too difficult to pronounce. I patiently waited for Eric to tell me the name.

After a long pause he asked "Are you there?"

I replied with a quick robotic like "Yes."

"You're never going to believe who it was; I almost had a heart attack." Eric said before hesitating to reveal the culprits identity.

Not one for suspense, I demanded "WELL, who the hell is it?"

"It was Rob Green. I don't know how they found out, but Trinoli said he saw the cops taking him out in hand cuffs during 4th period. A whole bunch of news stations are here and they have been trying to interview anyone who will talk to them. I even heard they might close school until everything is worked out." Eric said.

Almost dropping the phone I the only thing I could say was "Holy Shit!"

"And that's not it" Eric continued. "Apparently they found some journal or something in his book bag and it had all this crazy shut written in it and it talked about his plans for June 1st." He added.

"And you have no idea how school found out?" I asked.

"No, they won't say, but apparently he had written a list of names down, the names of who he was going to shoot. It's crazy man!" Eric went on.

"Who told you this?" I asked.

"Trinoli did, after he saw the cops arrest him, he went to Mrs. Madison's office and she told him everything."

"Holy shit Eric, I'm gonna go, I'll talk to you later." I said.

"Alright well if I hear anything else I'll let you know, I'll call you later." Eric replied before hanging up.

Many thoughts began to clog my mind. During the last two years I had many classes with Rob, and while it didn't come as a complete shock to find out it was he who was planning to execute his classmates, the news did startle me.

Rob was an extreme introvert and when he did talk he was sarcastic and cynical. He was the constant target of bullying and it started a long time before I had ever met him, and it was no different at Adams. He was regularly teased and ridiculed. Rob was heavy set with black curly hair, glasses and freckles and spoke with a subtle lisp. The first time I ever saw him he just sat at his desk and ignored classmates as they threw skittles at him, and I was one of them.

I have to be honest when I say that I have had a few encounters with Rob. During a Biology class one day when we had a substitute teacher teaching the class he uncharacteristically initiated a verbal altercation with me when he called my mother a whore. I never truly knew the reason he decided to pick a fight with me that day but after hearing the harsh insult I instinctively grabbed him by the collar of his shirt with both hands and slammed him into the wall. I warned him by saying "If you ever say that again, you'll be sorry. Do you understand?" He shook his head and I let go.

A few days prior to receiving Steve Garrett's letter, a verbal exchange that occurred between Rob and myself plagued my mind after Eric's phone conversation. Again we were in Biology class and the period was coming to a close as Dr. Schultz finished the day's lesson plan. A few of my friends and I were in a discussing the start of our playoffs in our basketball league. While Rob wasn't involved in our conversation I'll never forget his contribution. Still seated in his chair, sitting next one of his buddies, Rob looked in our direction and with a smug look on his face said "Sullivan you're dead and you don't even know it."

I looked over at him and loudly asked "What the fuck did you just say?"

Dr. Schultz, who was sitting at his desk reading a newspaper and drinking a black cup of coffee, overheard the volatile question and responded "WHOA!"

Unfazed by the teacher's acknowledgement of our conversation Rob maintained the serious look on his face with a calm approach replied "You dumb jock with your blonde hair and hoop earrings, your dad must think you're a fag. All you care about it is working out and playing sports. But it doesn't matter how much you can bench because you can't stop a bullet. You're dead; you just don't know it yet."

I guess that I have always been known to have a short fuse. I wasn't a confrontational person by nature but it only took a certain amount to set me off. Maybe it was a mixture of anger and fear of his threat that caused the explosion of emotions. At this point Dr. Schultz stood up from his desk and cautiously approached the situation.

There were two desks between Rob and myself and I grabbed the first and tossed in out of my way, like a bull my sight was set and I was seeing red. Now afraid, Rob stood up from his chair as his face turned white. Rob threw his arms up in defense. Before I could I toss the remaining table out of my way I was grabbed by Dr. Schultz, he wrapped his large arms around my shoulders and squeezed them tight. "STOP IT NOW!" he yelled in my ear, "CALM DOWN KEITH"

Unable to put thoughts into words I continued my pursuit but was unsuccessful. Dr Schultz was a large man and prevented me from reaching my ultimate target. When I was able to rely on speech rather than instinct I shouted "HE SAID HE WAS GOING TO SHOT, HE SAID HE WAS GOING TO SHOT ME."

"I don't think he was serious Keith." Dr. Schultz said. He then looked at Rob and said "I think you better leave now Mr. Green." Rob quickly collected his things and hurried out of the class room.

"HOW CAN YOU LET HIM GO?" I screamed, now trying to catch my breath. "He, he told me I couldn't stop a bullet. He, he said I was dead and I didn't know it. How is that not serious? This, this is BULLSHIT?" I exclaimed as my anger level began to rise once again/

"Watch your mouth or you're going to the principal's office." Dr Schultz responded.

"You're going to send me to the office for cursing, but you'll ignore a death threat? Are you serious? I continued to argue.

Dr. Schultz would make me wait in his classroom a few minutes after the bell rang. I was fuming and could not believe that this teacher would turn a blind eye to something as severe as a death threat especially with all that happened.

After the class I had stormed through the hallways for the rest of the day hoping to find Rob Green and but I never did. He must have skipped out early in fear that I was going to do something drastic. He did not come to school for the next couple of days, lying low at home while I cooled off.

That following Monday was the day when I received the threatening letter from Thomas Garrett. At the time it did not cross my mind that the two could have been linked but unfolding events would prove otherwise.

It was revealed that Rob Green had disclosed all of his plans and ideas to Thomas Garrett a few weeks prior to writing his threat on the bathroom wall. A few days before Rob's arrest, Thomas, who had kept the information a secret all this time no longer could keep it to himself and disclosed the information to his girlfriend Maggie. As the apparent plot began to weigh on the girl's conscious, she could no longer stay quiet and she did not want to feel responsible if a Columbine incident happened at Adams and she didn't warn anyone. Maggie told Tom that if he did not go to the principal or call the police to tell them what he knew that she would. When Tom did not respond to her request she felt that she had no other choice. On the morning of Rob Green's arrest, Maggie visited with Principal Cald and told him what Thomas Garret told her. Principal Cald quickly called the police and both Rob Green and Thomas Garrett where apprehended shortly thereafter.

As Rob was escorted to a nearby holding cell, Thomas was taken to the basement where he was previously interrogated for the letter he wrote for me. When questioned by the police why he did not come forward with his knowledge, Thomas said that he was threatened with his life if he were to tell anyone. He said that he felt that Rob was bluffing about the threat and was just having a little fun. He said Rob always talked things of this nature even before the Columbine incident. He said that Rob was all talk and that he wasn't the type of person to commit such a crime. Police officers told Thomas that his answers were not justifiable and that he put his life and the rest of the students at John Adams High School at risk. If Rob Green did follow through on his commitment Thomas would have been an accomplice and would be prosecuted in a court of law.

Thomas was almost expelled for his silence. I heard that he cried like a baby during his second interrogation with officer Gallagher. Principal Cald suspended Tom for a week with an additional two weeks of detention tacked on. Finally Principal Cald decided that it was necessary that once a week for the remainder of the school year Thomas Garret had to meet with Principal Cald to discuss "current events."

As for Rob Green, he was expelled from John Adams High School and was charged with a number of criminal felonies but he never saw a court room. Rob was under 18 and authorities felt that six months in juvenile detention and 250 hours of community service was a fair penalty. He would tell police and the school that it was just a prank and that he never intended to go through with it

Police Officers were granted the permission to search Rob Greens parent's house the day after Rob was arrested. What the officers found was intriguing. Robs father was an avid gun collector and he boasted a large locked showcase storing pistols rifles and shotguns. The showcase did not appear to be tampered with but upon review of Robs bedroom officers found a key duct taped underneath Rob's mattress. The hidden key just so happened to a be a duplicate to his father's prized showcase. This should have been evidence enough to charge Rob with some sort of criminal felony but juvenile detention with three years' probation was his punishment

To me at least, the most chilling revelation of all was that it was speculation that Rob was planning to start his shooting spree in his homeroom class, which Eric and myself shared. Both Eric and my name were on his list. These rumors were never backed up with any substantial evidence, but I heard they were started from Thomas Garret. Eric and I were consistently the first students to arrive in home room.

It was almost a year since I'd last seen Rob Green. One Saturday afternoon I stopped at a favorite fast food restaurant to grab lunch but instead I got something a little extra. Working in the window of the drive-thru was none other than Rob Green. He would hand me my order never realizing who I was. After pulling through the drive through, I parked in the first available space. Many emotions would race through me. A part of me wanted to rip him out of the window while the other wanted to ask him why. I never did get closure on the matter. Something's I guess we never supposed to know the answer.

You never really know what someone is capable of and fortunately for me I did not have to witness the power of his demonstration. Maybe I did not realize the effect that words and insults have over time on an individual. Everyone has their breaking point and we all react to or tormentors in a different way. You can only bottle up so much anger and frustration until eventually there is no room left for storage.

# Chapter 15:

There are certain people that you will come across that will forever leave an imprint in your life. My 12th grade history teacher was one of them. Mr. Harrison was indeed a character. He was our senior class advisor and extremely involved in all school activities. He had a unique teaching style and did not mind using unusual tactics to teach a lesson. Mr. Harrison was a bartender on the side, he worked at a local city owned franchise bar and grill Bingham St Brewery whose specialty were hot wings and signature beer that was brewed on the premises. Regulars at the bar called him bones. I made the mistake of saying the nickname aloud in class once and received a week's worth of extracurricular home work assignments

One Monday morning before class had started Frank, Eric and I was discussing the past weekend. Frank was a little upset with Eric. Eric's parents went away for the weekend and Frank took it upon himself to plan a party. Unfortunately for Frank, Eric decided to cancel at the last second and left his house on Friday night for Trinoli's. Frank considered Eric's actions insulting and that it was a blown opportunity for the perfect soirée.

"You're such a little bitch Eric. You had the house to yourself for the week and you bitched out." Frank argued.

"Yeah well I just didn't feel like cleaning my house by myself, you guys would have bailed man." Eric said defending his decision as he threw up his arms. When Eric spoke with a raised voice he normally used hand motions to support his claim

"Oh we would have help cleaned." Frank fired back in a sarcastic tone.

"Bullshit McAdams. There is no way you would have cleaned. Besides, you know my neighbor is a cop. He would have told me parents." Eric fought back.

"Oh come on Officer O'Malley is a drunk. All we have to do is buy him a six pack and he won't say squat." Frank pronounced. Frank had a way getting under your skin and he was succeeding in doing so with Eric.

"That's retarded." Eric said slamming his hands down on his desk.

"You're fucking retarded." Frank yelled.

Mr. Harrison was a little late coming to class and was walking into the room catching the end of their conversation. "What did you say Keith?" he asked.

"Excuse me, Mr. Harrison? I didn't say anything." I answered as I quickly looked over to Frank and Eric.

"Oh, well I must have not heard correctly. Let me see if I can reenact the conversation then." Mr. Harrison walks over to the chalk board picks up a piece of chalk and proceeds to write "You're Fucking Retarded," as he says it aloud while writing. Did I get that write Keith?

I didn't respond I just nodded my head. Mr. Harrison was insistent that it was I, not Frank, who spoke those words. I was waiting for Frank to interrupt Mr. Harrison and take responsibility, but he never did. If I were to plead my innocence it would only further upset Mr. Harrison and make my punishment that much stiffer.

"Because you feel the need to use inappropriate language and demonstrate such blatant disrespect for others around you I think that I have a little lesson for you Keith. On Thursday you will be assisting the special education class sell cookies instead of coming to my class. If you decide that you are not going to participate then you will be receiving an F for this marking period." Mr. Harrison proudly announced. He then began to go about his business and teach his scheduled lesson plan.

Frank looked at me as if he were about to say he were sorry and said, "At least you'll get some free cookies."

I ignored his comment and didn't speak to him for the rest of the day.

Every Thursday fresh baked cookies were sold out of the special education classroom. I usually stopped by if the line wasn't too long as the intoxication smell of baked chocolate lingered throughout the somber hallways of the first floor. This Thursday a lot of students were going to see me there assisting with the cookie sales. I don't know if it was Mr. Harrison's intention to embarrass me or humble me. All I knew was it should have been Frank there on Thursday.

Thursday had come and a couple of my classmates thought I was going to flake out. Mr. Harrison couldn't really get away with giving me a failing grade for not participating in the special education cookie sales could he? I was not willing to take the risk and see if he was bluffing. I was sure at some point he would stop by to see I was there.

The two women in charge of the special education class were Mrs. Carolyn and Ms. Albright. They were extremely upbeat women who displayed an exuberance of patience with their students. They were courteous to me and did their best to make me feel welcomed. I was nervous that Mr. Harrison's would disclose the real reason for participation. Instead I believed that he informed them that I was interested in volunteering.

Mrs. Carolyn and Ms. Albright thanked me for deciding to help out and introduced me to their students. As I met the boys and girls of the special education class I started to realize why Mr. Harrison sent me there. He was concerned about the lack of respect of other people's feelings. When we say things out loud we tend to be unaware that others may be listening and that are words can be offensive. Meeting these students had an emotional effect on me that I did not prepare for.

Two students in particular had taken a real interest in me Johnny Tambolin and Sean Myers. Johnny and Sean did not leave my side the whole time I was there and asked me many questions

"Do you play sports Keith, because I'm the football star?" Johnny said as he began to flex his muscles.

His question brought a smile to my face. "I thought you played football Johnny, you're a stud. I play well I used to play basketball." I answered.

Sean then jumped in front of Johnny and proudly stated "He's no football star, I am. Watch me tackle him."

The two started too playfully push each other around before Ms. Albright had gently asked them to stop horsing around.

As I was fretful that the woman would have me disturbing the cookies to patrons as they walked by but luckily for me I was responsible for placing the fresh cookies onto napkins. The period had almost gone by before Mrs. Carolyn had walked over and said "Excuse me Keith, but it seems that you have some visitors."

I walked over to the door and saw that Mr. Harrison decided to bring the whole class so that they could purchase some cookies and show some support. Mrs. Carolyn jokingly said to Mr. Harrison "I think we could use him every week." Mr. Harrison smiled and replied "We'll see what we can do."

Frank and Eric waited around after the class left to talk to me. Frank tried to score some free cookies but I wouldn't give him any. "Get any phone numbers?" Frank asked. I walked back into the classroom and left them in the hall.

A few minutes had gone by and I was beginning to help clean up as Ms Albright allowed a few students to venture over to the restroom across the hall. A moment after the students left to use the bathroom Sean ran back into the room and was out of breathe and hysterical.

"Some one lock the bathroom." He said "Everyone in the bathroom!"

About 10 feet down from the classroom was the designated bathroom for the special education students. It was a large bathroom that had a male and female section. I looked around the room and noticed that Johnny was not there, he must have been one of the students using the restrooms.

Sean grabbed my arm and pulled me into the hallway to show me what he meant He pointed to the bathroom before running back into the safety of his classroom. As I peered down the hallway it was now evident that another student was holding the door shut so that the students could not exit. He had both hands pressed against the door with his foot at the base. After a close look, I recognized him. His name was Louie Quinn. Quinn appeared to be enjoying himself as he laughed and taunted those trapped inside.

Quinn was a catholic school transfer who spent most of his time cutting class and sitting in the cafeteria or the art hall. He once skipped school for two weeks and started a rumor that he was killed in a car accident. No one really cared for the guy and there were actually a few people who were disappointed the story wasn't true. I never had any previous confrontation with Quinn, but I'm pretty sure he knew I didn't like him and he didn't care much for me.

"Son of a bitch." I said to myself. Quinn did not see me as he was far too impressed with himself. He continued to stand there laughing, unaware of the consequences that were about to happen. Quickly, I ran toward his direction and tackled him to the ground. He never saw it coming and I made clean contact with the lower portion of his upper body. As we hit the ground the force had slammed his head violently onto the floor temporarily knocked him unconscious. Blood began to flow from his nose.

The teachers had yet to exit the classroom and it was just Quinn and I alone in the hall. The situation quickly escalated out of control. I had severely injured another student and would be in serious trouble if a teacher were to see me.

Its funny how things have a way of working themselves out. I would have not been in the situation if Frank would have acknowledged his responsibility and told Mr. Harrison the truth.

It turned out that Frank never went back to class and was waiting for me so that he could thank me for taking the heat, as he was worried Mr. Harrison would have given Frank a more severe punishment. Frank was leaving the men's room and saw me on top of Quinn. Frank raced down the hallway and attempted to pull me off of Quinn.

"Go back in the classroom Keith; tell the teachers I did this. I owe you one man." Frank said quickly. I looked at Frank with a confused look. I didn't quite understand what he was saying as my adrenaline was still pumping from the hit on Quinn. "You heard me god damn it. You wouldn't have been in this mess if it weren't for me. Now get out of here." he demanded.

I listened to his request and I slowly stood up and walked back to the classroom. Ms. Albright and Mrs. Carolyn were still attending to Sean, who now had trouble completing sentences. The women thought he meant he was locked in the bathroom. I interrupted them to tell them Quinn had locked a few of their students in the handicap bathroom. The two women's calm quickly demeanor unraveled as they stormed out of their classroom and into the hallway. I followed.

At this point the three trapped students had made their way out of the restroom and were proceeding back to class. Frank was standing over Quinn who was still a little hazy Frank looked at the women and proudly stated "This asshole was locking your students in the bathroom...I apologize for my brash behavior but I have an Uncle that is handicapped ... and I uh, I guess when I saw him holding that door shut it just struck a nerve."

The women appeared to be grateful of Frank's actions and ironically enough seemed to have no interest in Quinn's physical condition. I wouldn't have been surprised if one of them spit on him.

"What kind of an animal torments handicapped children?" Ms. Albright asked.

Quinn, still dazed, looked up at the two women and replied "Huh?" Blood dripped from his face onto his clothing. He still lay on the floor as he attempted to recollect himself. "What happened?" Quinn asked himself.

"You were trapping these poor kids in the bathroom and laughing like it was some big god damn joke Quinn." Frank snapped.

Quinn turned his head back and saw Frank angrily peering over him. The two had a history. Before they both transferred to Adams, Frank & Quinn played soccer for rival catholic high schools. They had a few off-field incidents but this was their first confrontation now being students at the same school. Since transferring over to the Public school system, Quinn grew his jet black hair into a miniature sized Mohawk and sported a nicely pierced left nostril. He had a deep horse voice from the Marlboro red cigarettes he smoked frequently.

Frank was not lying about his Uncle. Well, technically I guess. His Uncle Ted spoke with a severe stutter and was a little slow, not exactly what you would consider mentally disabled but he faced some adversity in his life.

Strangely enough Frank received no real consequences for "his" actions. The Principal did, however, suspend him for a week for attacking another student. His intentions were deemed "those with the highest moral and ethics." He took full credit for my actions just as he would have taken full responsibility if those actions resulted in any legal measures. Quinn never pressed charges on Frank, it was rumored that Principal Cald informed Quinn that such actions would result with expulsion. Principal Cald did not want any more negative publicity for his High School.

# Chapter 16:

At the time it was the single most important piece of mail that I had received in my short life. I didn't expect to see it so soon but it was there never the less. I couldn't wait long and I quickly tore open the letter and read its contents.

*Dear Mr. Sullivan,*

*Thank you for interest in Penn State University and taking the time to complete the application process, however, we regret to inform you that we will not be accepting you for enrollment for the 2001 Fall Semester.*

*We have received a large number of applicants for the upcoming year and can only accept those with the highest of credentials. While your application was impressive, it does however lack in certain areas in which we hold in high regards.*

*Again, we appreciate your interest in Penn State University, and we wish you the best in your pursuit in higher education and all future endeavors.*

*Sincerely,*
*Admissions Director*
*Penn State University*
*Brian Flynn*

The letter was initially hard to grasp. It had to be a joke right. I had good grades, a decent S.A.T. score. I mean my mom made me take it three damn times. I participated in after school activities, played sports I was involved almost everything at John Adams

High school, what more could they be looking for, I thought. I had to get in to Penn State, I didn't apply anywhere else. What was I going to do? I began to grow afraid for my future.

"Well, what did it say?" My mother asked as she walked in the room, as the letter still remained in my hands.

"WHAT?" I replied, as I was not paying attention.

"The letter from Penn State, what did it say? Did you get in?" She said with a little more excitement in her voice.

"No." I said in a quick low voice as I looked down to floor. I placed my hands on my head and closed my eyes wishing for my mom to leave the room so I could be alone.

"WHAT?" she emphatically replied.

"NO I SAID. NO I DIDN'T GET IN!!" I screamed, taking out my frustrations on her simple question. "HERE, take a look for yourself" I said as I handed her the letter.

She quickly read the letter and quietly said "I'm sorry Keith, I really am," as the tone in her voice then changed slightly. "But, you don't have anyone to blame but yourself. I told you time and time again that you need to put more effort in your studies. You think you ever have to do is just show up and you'll be fine. You didn't want to take that pre SAT course that your father and I signed you up for. You said you didn't need to take it and look at your score: a 1080. You get B's when you should get A's and you would if you just put in some effort ..."

"I don't want to hear this right now mom!" I protested.

"Well you're going to hear it, YOU'RE the one who didn't get into Penn State, and you would have been shit out of luck if YOUR mother didn't send in applications to the other schools that YOU refused to apply too."

As I gave her a look of bewilderment she continued " ...And NO, it's not that I didn't think that you wouldn't get into Penn State, but you always have to be prepared Keith. You have so much potential and you're so smart, you just don't ever apply yourself and it's a shame."

As she said these words to me I became defensive. In the back of mind I knew that maybe she was right but I was young and I didn't want to admit it. No one ever wants to be wrong and I just thought I could take the easy way out.

I had a few options on the table. I could commute to a Penn State affiliate school for two years, keep my grades at a good GPA and hope to be able to transfer my junior year to main campus or I could attend one of the safety schools my Mom had applied for me. That is if I got in.

As my Mom began to continue her lecture, control was lost. "Just shut the fuck up Mom!" I yelled. "I don't want to hear anymore!" There is so much a person can take and although there was no one to blame for this rejection but myself, I lost my temper. My father was walking down the hallway, just finishing up showering when he heard the ill-timed words escape my mouth. I never saw it coming, but felt it immediately. My father had hit me above the temple and I stumbled a few feet and fell over the recliner. I covered up as he attempted to strike again. He hit me twice in the back before my mother grabbed his right arm and screamed "That's enough, Stop! Stop it Keith, STOP IT NOW!"

Reluctantly he backed off with my mother's hands still grasping his arm. I slowly stood up and quickly vacated to the safety of my room and slammed the door behind me. My parents did not permit us to lock the door, so they had the locks removed when I was 13. I slid the bed down the wall so that it would block any attempt to open the bedroom door.

I never saw my father so angry and I never spoke to my mother in such a classless demeanor. In fact I rarely ever heard my father speak in a profane manner. He rarely ever cursed and if you did hear use abusive language it was a good idea to get out of his way. About 15 minutes or so later I heard him storm down the hallway and attempted to open the door but found the blockade. "Open this door right now!" He demanded as I then pulled the bed back to its original position and my father entered my bedroom.

A fiery look still emanated from his eyes, he raised his hand and as he pointed to me and said "Don't you ever talk to your mother like that again, not after everything she does for you, 'cause let me tell you boy, you're lucky you have her. If it were up to me, things would be a lot different around here, a lot different." Before I could apologize he left the room slamming the door behind him.

Shortly thereafter Mom knocked on the door and asked "May I come in?" Before I could answer her she opened the door and had three envelopes in her hand. "I was waiting to give this to you until you heard from Penn State. I was hoping I didn't have to give these to you, but here they are. I didn't open them."

As she turned to walk away I said "Mom, I'm sorry."

"You better be" she replied, and then she left the room.

As it turned out I got into every one of the colleges that "I" applied too. I was not going to go the community college route and work my way into main campus and waste 2 years of the "college experience." The decision came down between two schools, Temple and Montgomery University. Temple was in the heart of the city, unfortunately not the best of locations, but was an excellent University and I would receive a sound education. Montgomery University was the second largest state school and was located 60 miles to the west. Although I was disgusted by the rejection of my first choice of colleges I was extremely thankful to have other options.

Later that day my father would apologize for hitting me but again reminded me to never speak to my mother in the way that I had. He gave me a pat on the back and said "I'm sorry that you didn't get in the school you wanted Keith. We don't always get what we want, but as you grow older you will find that you usually get what you need. Everything will be okay."

As soon as Dad left my bedroom I quickly dismissed his pearls of wisdom. Parents always have a way of telling you things that you don't want to hear.

My father always said "You'll understand when you get older," and I always felt that he meant I was too young too naïve to identify the meaning behind the story. Maybe that was true to a certain extent but it wasn't until I started to experience life for myself that I began to believe he actually knew what he was talking about.

# Chapter 17:

As a teenager, especially, we find that we gain enjoyment at the expense of others. It is a staple of human nature as it is hard ignore entertainment in its purest form; unfiltered and authentic. Certain events transpire throughout the course of the day where onlookers cannot help but indulge. Curiosity can sometimes get the better of us.

It was the start of spring and there always seems to be a change of attitude accompanies the transition of the seasons. It might be the pheromones or pollen, I'm not quite sure, but there is something about the return of warm air that "rejuvenates" us.

Unfortunately on this particular spring day, the weather decided to no cooperate as it was raining. It was 2nd period and we were enjoying our lunch period as usual just like any other day. I was just wrapping up my second platter when it started. (I was a growing boy, one lunch left me grumpy around 1) Something that initially seemed to be nothing more than minor exchange of words escalated quickly into something much greater. Our Lunch table sat in the bottom left corner of the lunch room along the back wall, we sat at this table for the last two years, and this year we added a table directly to the left which sat in the middle section of the cafeteria.

The table directly behind us, or in front of us, depends on where you were facing (as I have one said, life is truly about perspective) sat a bunch of what you would call "out-cast" students. They were the rebellious type of teenager. Many of these students were dressed in dark colors and there T-Shirts displayed vulgarity filled slogans. Their appearance screamed "I want attention," and their attitude conveyed individuals who wanted to be left alone. These "Freaks," as they were labeled at John Adams, listened to profanity laced anti-social inspired music and had open disregard for the status quo. They were proud of their stance, and most people left them alone, but they weren't without ridicule. I used to wonder how parents ever let their son or daughter leave house in such a manner, but some parents just don't give shit I guess.

Normally after eating lunch the "freaks" migrated from the cafeteria to congregate outside in the courtyard where they would smoke cigarettes and marijuana. During lunch periods, students were permitted to spend their time in what looked like a prison yard to get fresh air and "socialize." A 15 foot tall fence topped with barb-wire kept any student trying to escape there confides, as if they couldn't just walk out any of the unguarded doors around the school. Students who were regulars of the court yard had no intention of learning. For the most part they'd rather skipping classes and get high. Why come to school to do these things? For a school that boasted security, they didn't do a great job from keep outside teenagers from entering the building, and those who were monitoring the hallways to "ensure" safety were old women with walkie talkies. There were no real security measures taken to watch the cafeteria, where many free loaders enjoyed their day. There were maybe 2-4 uninterested security guards watching the exit and entrance doors to the lunch room. With all the students coming and going as they pleased, there was no way of knowing if they were scheduled for lunch that particular lunch period, or if they were even students of John Adams High School.

On this particular day it was raining, anyone who would have been out in the courtyard was forced to be restrained in the cafeteria.

A student by the name of Ryan Fox was sitting at the end of this table, which on this day was straight across from where I was sitting. More often than not we hardly ever paid attention to the table, but this was not Ryan's designated lunch period, and his presence had stood out.

A couple friends of mine had an encounter with Fox a few weeks back. They were getting dressed in the locker rooms, below the school's gymnasium, as they were getting ready for Phys Ed. A good buddy of mine, Mike Trinoli, noticed Ryan drawing something onto one of the lockers, and Trinoli found it offensive.

Trinoli was half Italian and half Jewish and if you didn't know him, you wouldn't have thought he was anything but Italian. His nickname was Balboa, as he looked nothing like the immortal "Rocky." He had thin light brown hair and hazel eyes which were accentuated by his dark complexion. He was a tremendous athlete at Adams. Trinoli was a punt returner/defensive back for the football team and was a star on the Track Team. Trinoli was very popular at Adams. There wasn't a student who didn't know him by name.

Trinoli walked over to Fox and saw the words "Jew Stomper" written in large black magic marker. Enraged, Trinoli steadfastly asked Fox "What the hell do you think you're doing?"

Fox turned around, shot Trinoli a filthy look and snapped back "What do you care, *you ain't a Jew.*"

Trinoli took a step closer to Fox, placed his hand in his shirt and pulled out the gold chain. Fox saw the Star of David proudly worn around Trinoli's neck. Trinoli wasn't known to pronounce his heritage, but the Jewelers he dangled in the face of Fox was a gift from his mother, and he wore it on occasion to appease her.

The expression quickly departed from Fox's face. "Well … are you going to stomp me? Aren't you going to stomp me then motherfucker?" Trinoli barked. Trinoli's normal laid back demeanor evaporated quickly in the dim dark catacomb like locker room. His fists were clenched tightly and his face grew red. Before any drastic measure could be taken, Fox grabbed his things and quickly left, as he was alone and outnumbered. Fox escaped further confrontation that day, but today, he would not be as lucky.

On this particular day Fox continued his creative approach as he carved something a little bit different on the lunch room table. A black student by the name of Jamaal, a student whom I have never seen before this day, was walking on his was to join his friends, as he approached Fox. Jamaal was about 10 feet from where Fox was sitting as he got closer he began to slow down. Fox and Jamaal crossed eyes quickly, and Fox jumped up from his seat. There no doubt that Fox's artistic addition to the lunch table caught Jamaal attention. A brief moment of silence passed as the two sized each other up.

The large confines of the cafeteria at John Adams were shaped in the form of a rectangle with three rows of lunch tables spread across what was comparable to the length of a football field. There were four entrances along the two front corners of the lunch room. Along the back perimeter of the cafeteria was the food and drinks were sold. There were four individual U shaped counters were different assortment of food was prepared for student consumption. The school offered Pizza, Hoagies, Chicken Nuggets, Burgers and other specialty foods on a daily basis, and for the most part the food was pretty good.

Fox wasn't that tall, standing around 5'9" but he was stout and today was dressed in radical army fatigue. He sported a shaved head and gangly facial hair. Jamaal was tall, lanky and slender. He was wearing baggy jeans with the trademarked timberland boots and a white t-shirt. He had a neatly trimmed goatee and a fresh fade hair cut.

Fox broke the silence by snarling "What the fuck are you looking at?"

Jamaal had no response. He just looked down at the table and shook his head at the swastika that was freshly carved into it.

Ryan had repeated his previous question "What the fuck are you looking at?"

Jamaal looked up and now directed his vision to Fox's eyes, still he said nothing. I cannot possibly imagine what was going through Jamaal's mind, but none of it was positive. Jamaal briefly turned his vision towards the table were his friends were sitting, who by now garner the attention of what was going down between Jamaal & Fox.

At this point one of Jamaal's friends who was been walking behind him, who had stopped to flirt with some girl, finally caught up. Brahir stopped in his tracks and saw the look of intensity portrayed on Jamaal's face. Ryan Fox, now engaged in a staring match with Jamal, balled his fists. For whatever reason, Brahir decided to walk down to the end of the table where Fox's friend Ethan was now standing as well, who just finished his own swastika. Ethan was much taller than Fox, but more slender. He too had a shave head, but had a baby face. He had an eyebrow ring above his left eye and his crystal clear blue eyes made him seem rather out of place with his cohorts. Brahir was dressed in similar attire to that of Jamaal. He was a bit larger with broad shoulders and a shaved head as well. He had neatly trimmed beard and a visible tattoo on his forearm. He also has a darker complexion and was more intimidating a force as he eyed up Ethan.

Ethan removed head phones from his ears as Brahir approached like a Tiger. Ethan & Fox were unaware of the bomb that they had willingly deployed. After Brahir's quick examination of Ethan's artwork, he makes eye contact with a now startled Ethan as the staring match between Fox and Jamaal evolves.

Jamaal calmly utters to Fox "Just say it."

The bomb reaches its target, our table watches with anticipation as we now prepare for the nuclear winter.

With the two still ten feet apart, Jamaal raised his voice and again says "Just say it, you cracker."

Fox mistakenly fires back "Fuck You Nigger!"

Not one second after Fox's words does Brahir reach back with great resolve and relentlessly slap Ethan across the face. The sheer force of hit sends Ethan flying to the wall and then to the ground. The sound echoed throughout the cafeteria and the volume of the blow was incomprehensible. Students flew from across the other end of the lunch room began to run over to get a better view. Ethan, who was still positioned on ground, became vulnerable to a barrage of hits to head. Ethan covered up his head the best he could and crouched into what appeared to resemble the fetal position

Fox's attention was drawn to his desperate friend. Jamaal saw his opportunity and quickly landed a jaw numbing strike that sent Fox towards our table, but he wasn't down. As he was dazed, he still managed to attempt to fight back. He took a swing at Jamaal and was unsuccessful. He did manage to grab a hold his Jamaal's shirt but help was already on the way.

Brahir left his excursion with Ethan to join his friend in combat. As Fox still had a hold of Jamaal clothing, Brahir followed up with a devastating punch that laid Fox out onto our lunch table. Fox was now helpless and a whirlwind of black students took turns at punching him.

It was unlike anything I had ever witnessed, I have seen a few fights but this was unrenowned. It was brutally organized and performed in sync like it was practiced. An upwards of 15 different students got their chance to hit the now lifeless Ryan Fox before any security officer could or would attempt to break up this riot.

By the time anyone tried to stop these enraged students, Ryan Fox now lay on the floor, in his own blood, and he was unconscious. Ethan received far less serve of punishment and was able to walk away with a cut underneath his left eye and some bruises to his face. Security officers now flooded the cafeteria but the damage was already done. Two students were detained by the school's security; police officers were on their way along with paramedics. The mêlée had left us speechless. Fox lay motionless on the floor, the spectators still yelling and screaming as school official's frantically struggle to restore order.

Perhaps the most memorable fact of the whole incident was that not one single friend of Fox or Ethan had interceded during the fight. Their peers, who most likely shared the same feelings on racial matters, sat quietly with their head downs as their comrades were brutally beaten in front of them. They did not say a single word during the whole incident, and a few of them were punched as well as they sat and did nothing. An image that reappears in my mind is this enormous man-child, who was sitting right next to Fox, was grossly larger than any other student involved in the fight that looked like an NFL offensive linemen, did nothing to help his "friend."

We were ordered out of the cafeteria with minutes to spare left in our lunch period. The whole ordeal was an out of body experience. Screen play writers could not have constructed a more surreal scene as it felt that you sitting in a theatre watching the finale to an epic battle between good and evil. And as I was not involved in this mess I soon would be.

The rest of the day seemed to just slide on by and classes melted into the other. The only topic of conversation between student and teacher alike, I had ringside seats for.

The funny thing of it was, and not that this was a laughing matter. No one had felt any real sympathy for Fox or Ethan. I mean how could you? They were "skin head" wannabes who deliberately displayed their hatred of others in a broad spectrum. Their decisions resulted in brash consequences.

The school that was said to be the "melting pot" of the city was beginning to boil over its stainless steel lid. Students weren't really integrated together as much as John Adams faculty and staff would lead you to believe. Areas of the school were sectioned off for more "gifted" students, while the confines of the dingy dirty basement level educated the students that didn't really care. English, Science and Math were taught on the top floors of the school, while gym and technical classes were on the lower floors. I don't need to go into great detail of what location you could find a certain student, but the only real interaction between "classes" was in the cafeteria and this is where you could run into trouble.

It seems to me that for too long we have been led down a narrow path and shown only one way of life. We seem to fear what we cannot explain it and we despise it because it challenges our mind and the process of thought.

Being a student at Adams introduced you to a world of diversity. An environment that promoted equality had turned into one that endowed hostility and violence. The aftermath could not be swept under the rug. The event would attract unsolicited media attention, constant police surveillance, enraged and paranoid parents, an unsettled student body and an anxious faculty and staff.

Tension was high and it could be seen building through the hallways by disgruntled looks and body language. Matters would not be forgotten, especially for those who witnessed the event. Three black students were arrested as a result of the brawl and were still in prison. Ryan Fox lay unconscious in a hospital bed fighting for his life.

Students who frequently paraded through the school's "art hall" section, where Fox spent a lot of his time, would make sure their voices was heard. They left a strong message for those black students who had sent their friends to the hospital. Those who had not the courage to voice their opinion the previous day, decided to strike in the shadows, a more convenient way of fighting back.

Early the next morning the art hall hallway was littered with thousands of cotton balls. A large sign was posted on the wall above that read "Go back to your roots Niggers!" The poster also presented its viewers with the initiating symbol, the swastika. Their retaliation was not taken lightly as students were no longer allowed to congregate in the art hall while security guards were to be posted in the area at all times during the day. The deed remained nameless and feed fuel to the already blazing fire that would prove far too difficult to extinguish.

Due to the size of the building, patrolling the hallways would become a difficult task. Small fights would break out throughout the school. Small gangs of black students would target any students perceived to be racist or involved with cotton ball situation and start a fight and some white students would be jumped just because. During the course the next few days there would be seven arrests and three students would be sent to the hospital. There were simply not enough officers to prevent every breakout.

Floods of reporters were located outside of John Adams and they were itching to obtain any information they could get their hands on. On the cover of the Daily News displayed a picture of the front of our school with the headline "School or Prison?" Adams was criticized because of the prison style bars on the outside of every window of the building, the barbwire on the fences and the riots that was taking place inside. An article now describes Adams as a "melting pot of races and ethnicities with certain ingredients just don't mix."

Reporters impatiently stalked the streets outside with hopes in they could entice students with 15 minutes of fame and garner an interview. Faculty, staff and students were asked to not cooperate with the media. The school could not endure any more harsh attention and with the ongoing events additional stories would surely keep the fire burning. Ignoring the school's wishes a number of students leaked information to the press, as those television cameras were quite enticing.

A fellow classmate Chris Gagnon decided that he wanted a little face time for himself. Gagnon was the school's Treasurer of the student body until he was forced to "resign" from the position after he was caught smoking marijuana on school premises. He was never arrested or charged with possession of illegal drugs because of his apparent relationship with Dr. Brodrick and the fact he was a student athlete. The issue just sort of faded away after he was only stripped of his duties, what a harsh penalty.

Gagnon was tall, outgoing and extremely cocky. He had light spiky blonde hair with blue eyes. We played basketball together in 10th grade and he was a pitcher on the baseball team. He was popular and disliked by many at the same time. We weren't particularly close friends but he was funny and I didn't practice the habit of burning bridges.

A few days after the "Race Riot," Gagnon grabbed me and said "We're getting on TV." We subtly walked out the front door and made a B line to the awaiting reporters.

"We were eye witnesses." Gannon exclaimed to a rather attractive red headed female reporter who had recently wrote a two page cover story about John Adams "A System in Turmoil."

"We saw it all." Gagnon continued.

Instinctively the reporter swarmed over to us and asked "What was it like being up close and personal when these events unfolded?" Gannon calmly replied "It was crazy; it was seriously like taken right out of the movies. It just happened so quickly."

Quickly the reporter followed with "What is the atmosphere now like in your school?"

"It's a little hectic; teachers are doing their best to control the students but its

rough ya know." Gannon responded.

She asked a few more redundant questions and Gagnon did all the talking. I began to regret the decision of coming out to talk to these piranhas. They didn't concern themselves with all the turmoil that plagued the school. They were worried about their next story.

"Well gentleman you take care and be careful." The reporter concluded as she offered a phony smile and jotted down some notes before discussing them a colleague.

Gagnon and I proceeded to walk back into the school when Gagnon looked at me and said "You stay with me and you'll go places, it's not what you know but who you know." He said with a wink.

# Chapter 18:

Almost two week after the appalling events, Ryan Fox still lay in a coma and three black students were in custody awaiting a potential trial, two of which were not Jamaal or Brahir. Things seemed to have settled down but they were by no means back to normal. A phone call would ultimately change this perception.

It was the beginning of fourth period and I was sitting in my psychology class. Class room telephones rarely ever rang. Students know this to be a fact. Unless the information was urgent, messages were normally left in person. When a teacher did receive a phone call, chances were a student was being called down to the office.

Professor Gavin's phone rang after the period began. It took him a little while to get to the phone as Mr. Gavin suffered from Polio at a young age and lost the use of his legs. There was a great deal of tension as Mr. Gavin slowly made his way to the phone as I had growing feeling in the pit of my stomach. Somehow I knew that this phone call was for me.

As he picked up the phone he said with a humorous tone "Hello?" A few seconds had gone by and Mr. Gavin responded "Yes, he is here … I'll send him down." Mr. Gavin hung up the phone and looked at my direction. "Hey O'Sullivan, you're wanted downstairs in the office, so get your stuff and get out of here." He always called me by O'Sullivan.

"Do you know what for?" I asked as I stood up.

"You finally did it this time, you're done." He answered with a smile. "Honestly

I'm really not sure, they didn't say."

As I made my way down to office I couldn't help but wonder why I was being summoned to the office. While walking down the stairwell I to ran into Mike Trinoli. As Trinoli noticed me a big smile emerged on his face. "What's up Keith, where are you going?" He enthusiastically asked.

"I was called down to the office. I'm not sure what for." I replied.

"Really? You think you're in trouble?" He curiously inquired.

"Yeah I probably am." I sarcastically said with a smile. "What are you doing? Taking a tour of the building?" I asked, changing the subject.

"No I'm just hanging out. I don't have to go to 4th period anymore Mr. Roal is a baseball fan, he comes to every game so, I just get a study guide before tests and I'm set." Trinoli proudly stated.

"Oh well good for you, I'll see you later man." I said.

"Good luck, I hope you don't get arrested." Trinoli jokingly said.

I shook my head in disbelief. It an unspoken rule, but student athletes catch a break by certain teachers. Unfortunately we didn't have many basketball fans, at least my teachers weren't. Trinoli didn't need any assistance; the guy could talk his way into or out of anything. He is the only person I know that could leave his house with five dollars and come back with twenty.

When I entered the office I immediately recognized the security guard who was waiting my arrival, it was Officer Gallagher. Once I walked in he quickly approached me and escorted me down stairs to the schools security headquarters.

"What's this all about?" I asked the large, silent, emotionless officer.

"You'll find out soon enough kid." He snapped.

Officer Gallagher had an extremely unyielding demeanor. Maybe it was the nature of his occupation that caused him to be so rather unpleasant.

"Thanks." I sarcastically answered right back.

"The problem with you kids is that you think you know everything and you don't know shit." He said under his breath as we continued down the hall way. Day in and day out he had to deal with "know it all" teenage punks. I was in shock he cursed at me and I still had no idea what this was all about.

We reached our destination Officer Gallagher opened the door and escorted me inside. Patiently sitting in the room was Police Officer Justin Smeltz. Officer Smeltz quickly stood up and introduced himself and gave me a firm, hearty handshake. He was burly man who appeared to be in his mid 40's. He was of average height, had a lightly trimmed beard, green eyes and jet black hair. He seemed eager to meet with me and had appeared to have a reserved demeanor.

"Good afternoon Keith, I am Officer Smeltz. You have been called down here today to help assist us in our ongoing investigation of the incident that took place March 15th. I am one of the lead investigators on this case and we would gladly appreciate any information you would be able to provide us with. So please, sit down son."

Officer Smeltz stood until I was seated. I did not get a chance to respond, as soon as the officer sat down he said "Now Keith, for the last few days we have been compiling footage that was filmed in the lunchroom before, during and after the incident. We have confirmed with our film and your current class schedule that you were in fact present during this altercation. Am I correct with this information?"

I hesitated at first and then responded "Yes Sir."

Officer Smeltz continued "Good. Okay. We will be extracting the statements of a few other individuals whom were present and comparing them with your statements. Now if you could for me please, explain to me what exactly happened? And please be as detailed as you can, take your time."

Officer Smeltz took put pen to paper and waited for my testimony. I explained to him the intensity of the situation and the manner in which the incident had quickly escalated, it was hard to remember every detail. I tried to be as thorough as I could, unfortunately we would disagree on such information. I was immediately stopped and shown a picture of each of the three students that were in custody; one in particular, Eric Byers, was being charged for attempted murder of Ryan Fox. I was quite familiar with Eric. He was friends with a few of the guys on the basketball team. He came to practices and games. Eric never threw a punch. To be honest with you I can't even remember seeing him in the lunch room that day.

I protested that Eric had nothing to do with the fight. Officer Smeltz indicated that they had Eric on film and he was present. Apparently Eric was the only student who was recognized on camera that had a criminal record. Eric was 18 and could be tried as an adult. The police had no leads, the film was less than adequate to pinpoint who was where (except for me obviously.) Maybe Officer Smeltz was following the chain of command and higher ranking officers breathing down his neck for a conviction, but Eric Byers was not guilty.

"If it wasn't Eric, than who started the fight?" Officer Smeltz groaned.

"I don't know who they were, I never saw them before." I responded.

I was referring to Jamaal and Brahir. Those weren't really their correct names, I didn't make them up to protect them in anyway. I just didn't know them. Officer Smeltz was unable to offer any pictures of them so I was unable to point them out for him.

"Well that seems a little to suspicious to me son, who are you trying to protect here?" Officer Smeltz demanded.

"You don't understand officer you weren't there, it just happened so fast, before I realized what was going on it was almost over. I'm not trying to protect anybody. Ryan Fox was carving a swastika into the table and called a black student a nigger. I'm not prejudice or a racist but Ryan Fox deserved it. I cannot sit here and let someone who is innocent go to jail for something they did not do. It's not fair" I stated.

"Hey kid, life isn't fair. It never has been and it never will be and you need to get used to it. If Eric Byers did not kick Ryan Fox in the head, then who did?" Officer Smeltz questioned.

The images started to again play in my head and for the life of me I did not remember anyone kicking Ryan Fox at all. "No one did officer. A whole lot of guys punched him when he was on the table but I don't remember him being kicked." I exclaimed. I began to feel defensive as the officers tone gradually intensified and he was not accepting my answers as accurate.

"Mr. Sullivan, the tapes don't lie. When school officials and security guards FINALLY attempted to end this quote-unquote "race riot" as the newspapers have so eloquently titled this, Mr. Fox was down on the cafeteria floor. After clearing all the students from the lunchroom the school officials did not move Mr. Fox until paramedics arrived on scene so that they could ensure that proper measures were taken so that there would be no further injury to Mr. Fox. In instances such as this, there is always the fear that the victim has suffered possible neck trauma. Fortunately, in the case, the result left Mr. Fox in a coma but not paralyzed. SO AGAIN, I will ask you Mr. Sullivan. WHO kicked Ryan Fox as he lay on the cafeteria floor?" The Officer demanded.

I hesitated for a moment and tried to collect my thoughts, "Sir, I'm sorry, but I just don't remember. I am telling you everything that I know; I don't what else you want me to say."

"Son, I need you to tell the truth. The fact of the matter is there is a boy lying in the hospital and he is in a coma. One of your classmates has been brutally attacked and severely injured AND you my friend are an eye witness to this crime, with court side seats no less and you have the god damn nerve to tell me that you cannot remember a simple fact as to whether Mr. Fox was kicked in the head. If you are unaware of the severity of Eric Byers actions then I will inform you. The crime is regarded as assault with a deadly weapon and attempted murder. Last time I checked, that's a pretty serious offense. NOW, somebody has to pay for this crime. All of our leads in this investigation point to Eric Byers and he is going to be charged for the attempted murder of Ryan Fox unless you, or someone else for that matter, can tell me WHO did it" The officer passionately spoke.

"I wish that I could do that, I really do. All I can say is that Eric Byers is innocent." I answered

"If you feel so strongly about his innocence then you are going to have to testify in front of a judge and jury. Are you so sure you're willing to do that for some poor black kid from the inner city?" Officer Smeltz asked adamantly.

"Yes I am." I replied.

"Let me offer you a little bit of advice son. Now, I don't care if you think I'm an asshole or that I'm racist or prejudice or whatever else I have been called during my time here on the force. I used to be stationed in the heart of the worst part of this city and let me tell you I've seen one too many injustices occur that I care to remember. I've seen innocent men found guilty and guilty men let free and there ain't nothing that you or I can do about it. The system is flawed and people like you and I will never be able to change that. We have neither the power nor money that is required to execute change and this is something that I have come to accept. Now while your intentions are honorable, let me tell you something, we all start out with the best of intentions and then this world has a way of breaking you down and stripping you of your decency. Criminals are not born as crooks but they eventually become a product of their environment. Eric Byers is a criminal. He has a record and it is more than likely that he will commit another crime if let go. Now I can assure you that if the roles were reversed here, he could give a shit about you. I've checked his school records Keith; he hasn't passed a class since he transferred here. He ain't ever gonna graduate and he's gonna go back to his nigger neighborhood and push dope or better yet become a murderer …"

"You don't know that officer" I interrupted.

"Kids like that do not have a future, they poison our cities. I know that you're a ball player Keith; I know that you've seen this city in all of its glory. The blacks in this city call a white cop "pig" and a black cop "brother." And let me tell you something, if you were down a dark alley and Eric Byers had the opportunity to stop his homies from shooting you, he wouldn't, because blacks stick together. If you think one of 'em would stick out their neck for some "cracker" you've got another thing coming son. If Ryan Fox were some black kid and his adversaries' white, the reporters would have tagged this whole mess a Hate Crime. There'd be national news coverage. But John Fox is white and some neo Nazi skin head piece of white trash so no one gives a shit. Well I do! Because that's my job and it's my job to put scumbags like Eric Byers in prison. I'm not going to let some gang banging low life go free when he should be behind bars and off my streets. Do yourself and your city a favor kid, just say that Eric Byers is guilty. Because you do not want the negative attention that this trial will bring to you and you certainly do not want to testify in court. Just leave this matter in our hands and I promise you that justice will be served." He said.

I thought about what the officer had said and his words made me apprehensive about going to court but I knew I had to make the right decision. "Eric Byers is innocent and I'll testify in court." I said.

His eyes grew large and face slightly reddened "Well I'd like to thank you for cooperation Keith, you have been most helpful. You are free to leave, so go back to class." Officer Smeltz sarcastically said, slamming his hands onto the table as he stood up.

I bounced out of the cold uncomfortable chair grabbed my book bag and headed for the door. As I put my hand on the door knob and Officer Smeltz had one last thing to say. "You'll be hearing from us soon." The smile quickly evaporated from his face and his attention fell back into his notes as he jotted something down.

I left the room with more anxiety than when I entered it. I did not want to go to court and testify. I wanted this whole mess to subside, but I could not let someone be charged with a crime they did not commit. I was there and if my testimony would alter the outcome then that is what I had to do.

Officer Smeltz would interview two more students who had witnessed the fight. Both students gave similar statements and had indicated Eric Byers was not responsible. They too were told that they would have to testify in court. One student would agree to the date in court while the other student retracted their statement and agreed to Officer Smeltz demand and confessed Eric Byers was guilty.

# Chapter 19:

As the fate of those involved waited in the shadows, a dim light would shine the truth. Ryan Fox would wake from his concussion a few days after I was interrogated. His hospital room would be hounded by police and media alike, trying to have him reenact the gruesome scene and how his life had almost come to an end. Fox had no remorse or regret for his actions. When examined Fox arrogantly told police officers his version of the "Race Riot." The officers must have been stunned over Fox's words and his convictions.

I never once heard again from Officer Smeltz nor would I have to testify in court. All criminal charges were dropped against the alleged assailants. Eric Byers would not be charged with attempted murder. Ironically no one would be charged with a crime, it was like it had never happened. Fox was not reprimanded for his bigoted actions, while many thought he would be expelled from school. Apparently his hospital time served was viewed harsh enough a penalty. The NAACP would ultimately get involved in the matter, sending out a few representatives over to the school in a furious tirade trying to receive what they considered in their minds to be due justice. The decision made by the NAACP to further pursue involvement in the incident would continue to draw negative attention to our school and result in continued tension for students and teachers alike.

The NAACP would not stay very long as their representatives only visited a few days. The allegations were confirmed about Fox's involvement and he was finally expelled from Adams for his repeated racial conduct and instigating the "Race Riot."

The incident was in the rear view mirror. A few weeks would pass and there were no new stories written from the attention crazed journalists who had stalked Morris Avenue for breaking news. The visits from officials, politicians and organizations had ceased. School security was at an all time high and patrol cars frequently made their rounds around the schools perimeter. Principals Cald's character would be questioned for allowing such an event to take place under his supervision. At the end of the school year Vice Principal Andrew Chalmers would be asked to resign from his position. Mr. Chalmers was the school disciplinarian and in charge of security matters.

One of the major causes for criticism was the amount of time in which it took security and school officials to disengage the students and altercation. Someone had to pay, and Vice Principal Chalmers took the fall. He would find a vacancy in one of our rival high schools Roosevelt High School. Principal Cald managed to lure away one of Roosevelt's Vice Principals shortly after Chalmers resignation.

To appease the NAACP and revive the distinction that Adams was a school of multicultural learning and understanding, Principal Cald would permit the admission of African American students who was expelled from their prior schools. At a press conference Principal Cald would say "We at John Adams High School feel that every child deserves a second chance. Our institution of learning encourages and teaches all of our students to have an open mind and to accept the benefits of equality. We pride ourselves on our commitment to a multicultural learning environment that will brighten our city and children's future."

The irony here is that Adams did house a variety of ethnicities and races, but didn't excel at harboring students with the same ideals that Principal Cald was preaching. It easy to expect results without effort but it's idiotic to tell others of your success when your failures have just recently been on display for all to see. A school that boasted its equality seemed to fall in line with the rest of societies view on diversity, conceptual it's a great idea but we're not quite there yet.

# Chapter 20:

The next couple of months fly by. We get ready for the finale as we have concluded the infamous senior prom. A whole bunch of hype led up to what girls and boys wait for twelve years of education to participate in, and in all honesty, it was just another Friday night. We got dressed in tuxedos and gowns and danced as we drank soda and listened to pop music. The highlight of the night was when a student asked his pregnant girlfriend to take his hand in marriage.

We were now two weeks away from graduation and we just finished our final exams. We were officially on cruise control and just going through the motions. We skipped classes and frequently left the building during lunch and whenever else we wanted. The teachers didn't seem to mind much really, I mean what could they do? Our grades were already in.

It was a Thursday and we were all set for our Senior Picnic. The school had reserved a park/day camp in the suburbs for the festivities. Before we boarded the fleet of yellow school buses our yearbooks has been distributed. The buses were humming as everyone torridly examined high quality colored pages offered a plethora of pictures, quotes and memories.

Mike Trinoli, who was a known photo thief, on a number of occasions, was caught sweet talking his way into the year book office and "borrowing" photos. Trinoli recorded an astounding 22 pictures in our edition. We had joked that the editor had a serious crush on Trinoli.

We reached the park and handed each other our "memories" so that they could leave their insignia and heart filled paragraphs. The camp ground had an in-ground swimming pool, basketball and tennis courts, and pavilions for lunch and open fields that were off limits to the students. Barbeque grills were cooking hotdogs and hamburgers and coolers provided water and soda while there was a nice assortment of other "barbeque" related side dishes and snacks. The school really out did itself. I had to say that I was very impressed for the set-up.

As we sat, ate and enjoyed ourselves we looked at our yearbooks some more and discussed our future plans and were we would be attending school. The majority of our friends would be scattering around Pennsylvania attending State schools while a few were off to private and Ivy League Universities.

After lunch a few of the guys decided to play a pickup game of basketball. As we were picking teams Frank sat under the shade of a tree, lit up a joint specially rolled for the occasion, as he gave me a glance and said with a smile "Hey hot shot, I thought you quit?" I ignored his remark I sat on the concrete and stretched.

Before we had finished picking teams big time football star Bobby Jackson walked over and asked if he could play. Bobby had a scholarship with Maryland University to play linebacker. Bobby was a physical specimen. At 6'3, 235 pounds of muscle, it was hard to imagine someone that young being could be in such incredible shape. Bobby resembled a young Bo Jackson, from his build to the hair cut. He wore a gold chain around his neck and had two large diamond earrings in both ears. He was the only guy I knew at the time to wear an earring in both ears, and I doubt anyone ever questioned him about it.

"I heard you got some game Sullivan, I hear they call you Larry Bird" Bobby sarcastically said before we started.

A little competition never hurt anyone, but I would lie to you if Bobby wasn't intimidating. Running a few times up and down the court with Bobby guarding me I was able to see what a great athlete he was. He was fast and quick at the same time and though I didn't get to see it, I'm sure he could dunk with great ease. Five minutes into the game, however, an unfortunate injury would tarnish the day and Bobby's future.

I received the ball down low in the post from a bounce pass from Trinoli, I turned around to face the basket, gave a quick pump fake and Bobby reacted. The football star soared high into the air and landed awkwardly on the unforgiving blacktop. With all of his weight going to the right and foot twisting to the left, he dislocated his heel. It was an eerie sight watching our schools top athlete scream in agony. His foot pointed in the complete opposite direction that a foot is supposed to, it tilted almost sideways. Bobby's shoe was cut off to relieve some of the mounting pressure building on his ankle. An ambulance was called so that he could be taken to a nearby hospital.

Solemnly we watched as the ambulance pulled away. A sinking feeling sat in the pit of my stomach. I remember hoping that he would be okay.

As I sat on a park bench in shock, Frank walked over and put his hand on my shoulder and said "It ain't your fault man, shit happens."

He paused for a second "I'll tell you what I'm going to do, I was going to keep this a surprise until tomorrow, but I guess that I'll tell you now."

A sinister smile grew larger "My dad left this morning for New York and will be staying the weekend for a little "rendezvous" with some chick he met last month at some conference. So I'll be home alone. I already have the kegs on call, ice in the downstairs freezer and George Marshall's band waiting on speed dial. I figure it'll be a nice little pre-graduation party. You know something to tell our kids about."

Frank had an "I'm extremely proud of myself" look on his face.

"You never cease to amaze me Francis?" I said.

"Yeah, yeah I'm great I know. But now since I told you, I'm gonna need your help." Frank said.

"There's always a catch with you McAdams, this isn't let's make a deal, what do you need?" I asked.

"Well, since you asked nicely. Apparently my dad decided that before he left today he was going to take my credit card and debit card and leave me only a fifty freaking dollars to get through the weekend. He's treating me like some damn animal." Frank complained.

"Yeah, so, what would you like me to do about it?" I asked cautiously.

"Well" Frank said then paused for a second, carefully preparing his next words. "I was hoping that you would be willing to invest in the festivities." Frank hesitantly asked.

"Ha!" I laughed. "How much do you need?"

"My father was unaware of the Benjamin I had stashed in my closet, along with my recreational drug collection and paraphernalia ..."

"Yeah, you're father really needs to start drug testing you again." I interrupted.

Frank dismissed my comment and continued. "SO, that gives us 150 bucks for the party. I figure that I need to get at least 3 kegs, plus cups, a tap, food etc., etc. The cheapest kegs cost about $ 70, plus don't forget the deposit for the tap. We're roughly looking at around 220 for the beer alone. Plus I want to get a bottle of Jack Daniels for the guys and maybe some additional party favors. The way I figure it is, if we go 50-50, (starts to sing a Bob Marley tune) *every little thing is gon' be alright.*"

"Well. I guess so. Let's do it to it." I said. He knew I couldn't turn him down, especially not at the expense of our social lives. Frank had a few good parties in the past. I was hoping this one would be great.

Frank grew giddy and we slapped hands as he said with a large smile "My man pots and pans. I'm glad that you're in, because if you turned me down I would have told everybody you were the reason I had to cancel. And I knew you wouldn't want that hanging on your conscience." Frank said with a smile.

I shook my head and said "The sad thing is I know that you would have. Can I ask you a question though, why would you wait till the last minute to ask me?"

"I have a feel for the dramatics, and when everyone compliments me on what a great party I threw, I can brag that it only took me a day to set up." He said.

"The party that WE threw, you mean." I added.

"Yes and by I, I mean us. You should know this by now Sullivan." Frank responded. "Oh and by the way, since we are in this together, you're gonna have to run the front door."

"What?" I asked.

"Don't act so surprised, you know you're hired muscle. You don't have to do it the whole night, just when people start showing up. You know collecting money, giving out cups and kicking whoever I want out. You have my blessing to do whatever you want, besides you're getting paid … AND best of all, you'll get to show everybody how cool you are." Frank said.

"Thank you for the opportunity. And what may I ask will you doing?" I asked.

"I'm upper management. I'll be in my office doing drugs, counting money and having sex with multiple women." Frank quickly answered.

"Yeah, I've been meaning to talk to you about that buddy. Jeannette Matthews has been telling everyone that you were a little too quick on Prom night." I mockingly stated.

"Well, Jeannette Matthews fails to understand that what we do between the sheets is a game we play from time to time. And the object, my friend, of every game is to win. I finished first. Therefore I won. And believe you me I'm always the winner!" Frank proclaimed. "I'm going to go back and sit under that tree and make some phone calls for tomorrow night, but first would you like to join me while I finish this joint?"

"You know I don't smoke." I answered.

"Well it never hurts to ask." Frank said.

As I began to walk away Frank gave me a hearty slap on the ass and said "Good Game!" Always the character, he had a knack for saying the wrong thing and turning it around to be funny.

Frank possessed the quality of being carefree, never thinking twice about what others thought of him. He was who he was and was proud of it. He did not care who he offended and rarely ever apologized. He would say "Everyone is entitled to their opinion and I have no problem expressing mine."

He would often debate that we are too afraid to use their given right of freedom of speech. He would complain that people are afraid of the consequences of their opinions and individuality. That we live in a society of "Do as I say and not as I do," were we more worried about being politically correct than speaking the truth.

I was rather fascinated by his insight and views on society. His knowledge was impressive, considering the way he presented himself in school as a slacker. When a subject would get under his skin and he would begin to go off on a tangent and I would cool him down by referring to him as Senator. He would respond by saying "I'm too cutting edge to be a politician. I'd be assassinated or impeached within a month."

# Chapter 21:

Everything was ready and accounted for. I just got out of the shower and was in the midst of changing when I heard a knock on the door.

"May I come in?" asked my father.

"One second dad, let me put some clothes on real quick." I answered.

I put on some underwear and a pair of pants and said "Okay, come in." Dad walked into the room and shut the door behind him. He had a serious look on his face and I could only think "What did I do now?"

"I need to talk to you for a second Keith..," He started. "...you're brother tells me, that you told him he wasn't allowed to go to Frank's party tonight with you." Before I could interrupt he raised his voice a little "Let me finish. I know that he is a little younger than you and he looks up to because you're his big brother. I had younger brothers and my mom used to make me watch them and I always had to take them with me. It might feel like he is tagging along, but he is you're only brother. Blood is thicker than water Keith. Look at the relationship I have with your uncles, I don't want it to be like that with you and Derek."

"Okay Dad, I understand but it's a graduation party and I don't feel like looking after him tonight." I argued.

"Keith either he goes with you, or neither of you go! That's final." He declared. "I almost forgot, is Franks father is going to be there tonight?" He asked.

"Yes, Dad I told you before, Mr. McAdams is going to be there." I said agitatedly.

"So If I call his house, he will pick up?" He then asked.

"YES." I exclaimed.

"Hey, that's enough with the attitude. In one minute you'll be walking to Frank's while I drop your brother off. Understand?" He said.

"Yes I understand, but I have to finish getting ready." I didn't particularly enjoy lying to my parents, but they would have made a fuss if they knew Mr. McAdams wasn't going to be there. It was only a white lie, kind of.

My father left the room and shut the door behind him. "God damn it!" I thought. It's not that I hated my brother, but it's not like we particularly got along that well either.

As soon as I made sure my father was down stairs I stormed into Derek's room and said "Listen, I just talked to dad and he told me that you bitched about me not letting you go tonight. So congratulations! You're going." I didn't even give him the chance to respond before I stormed out of his room. Derek followed me out of the room into the hallway and gave me a push in the back. I nearly fell into the wall.

Stunned by his actions, I turned around to confront my little brother and there he stood with tears of anger in his eyes and his fists balled. "We're brothers Keith and you're friends are always more important than me. You act as if I were some embarrassment to you. I'm sorry that I'm not as cool or as popular as you are. I'm sorry that I think that you're funny. But if you keep this up, one day I won't be there, and you'll be sorry."

"I'm not embarrassed of you Derek. I just don't want to have to look after you. If anything were to happen, mom and dad would kill me."

"You don't have to look out for me. I am old enough to take care of myself. Forget about the "quarter" thing. That was so long ago."

When I was twelve years old I finally convinced my parents that I was finally old enough to watch after my brother and that we no longer needed a babysitter when they weren't home. I felt I was responsible enough to earn their trust and desperately wanted a little more independence. Besides it's not like they ever hired any attractive babysitters, only in the movies right?

My parents hadn't been gone an hour. They had left us some money so that I could pick up some pizza for dinner. I left their change on the dinning-room table when we got home from dinner. My parents always complained that I never gave back their change so this time I wasn't going to give them anything to complain about. I was on my best behavior because I did not want to give them any reason to take away this new found privilege and independence.

After dinner Derek was playing with one of the quarters from the remaining change lying on the dinning-room table. Derek had developed the disgusting habit of putting anything and everything into his mouth. He chewed on plastic, paper, pencil erasers. Just about anything he could manipulate to fit into his mouth he would chew, apparently even coins.

Derek put the quarter in his mouth and must have forgotten about it. We never really talked about it so I'm not certain of his explanation. A few minutes later he hiccupped or burped and the quarter slipped down his throat and was now stuck. Immediately he started coughing, causing the coin to further lodge itself in his throat and he began to choke. As his face turned blue he began to panic, wasting energy and the oxygen that was left in lungs.

I didn't hear him choking at first; I was sitting on the couch watching T.V. When I finally noticed what was happening his face was already now dark blue. There wasn't much time to react and luckily I was somewhat prepared. In health class they recently thought us the Heimlich maneuver. And here I thought that I never would have to use it. I quickly grabbed Derek and started pushing my fists under his rib cage. It took three tries before I could dislodge the coin. The quarter shot out of his mouth like a rocket. The color returned to his face as he gasped for air and fell to the floor. Before regaining complete composure Derek continued the excitement by vomiting all over the carpet. As the large red stain began to settle into our parent's new carpet, Derek looked up at me and asked for a glass of water. We desperately tried to remove the stain with every cleaning product that was stored in the kitchen and despite all of efforts the stain would remain permanent.

Of course, when my parents would come home I was blamed for Derek's near death experience and the irremovable remnants of pizza sauce. I guess it was my fault that Derek put the quarter in his mouth and I should have been watching him. The light red stain proved to be too much of an eye sore on their beautiful new beige carpet and it forced my parents to purchase a replacement after 5 months of its installation. I was grounded a week for "being irresponsible" and I was not allow me to be alone in the house with my brother until I was 15 years old. This is what I considered to be a crime against humanity.

The incident also resulted in two truths: I would never again take responsibility for my brother, and I would begin to resent him. I felt betrayed that he never came to my defense. Maybe he was still in shock that he almost died but that's not an excuse I was going to accept. I didn't put the quarter in his mouth and the little bastard never did thank me for saving his life.

"You talk about being brothers? I don't even trust you. You constantly rat me out to mom and dad for everything I do. When have I ever told on you for anything? We are nothing alike Derek. I love sports, and you hate them. I like to go have a good time with my friends, you'd rather study. You're quiet, I'm loud. We have nothing in common. I don't even know why you want to go tonight. You don't drink. You probably just want to go so that you will piss me off. You say we're brothers, I say we are barely friends and that's your fault." I said.

As tears continued to roll down his from his eyes, Derek was obviously hurt by my callous remarks "We used to be such good friends when we were younger. We did everything together and now you don't want anything to do with me. I just want to be friends again." Derek said before he walked back into his room like a dog with its tail between its legs.

As he shut the door behind him a sense of remorse resulted from the heated words that were exchanged. Instantly I realized my comments were harsh and somewhat cruel. I really did not mean them, but I had the habit of doing that, letting anger get the best of me. My temper occasionally forced me to say things that were not true but maybe it was time to let go of this grudge that I was holding in for so long. It was my time to be the bigger man and apologize.

I opened the door without knocking and entered Derek's bedroom. He was sitting on his bed with his head in his hands. He did not acknowledge me when I initially walked in and without lifting his head he softly said "Just leave me alone, Keith."

In a sincere tone I said "Derek, I am sorry about what I said to you, I hope that you know that I didn't mean it. I hope that you can forgive me...You are right. We used to be best friends. More importantly we are family and I love you." I sat down next him and put my left arm around his right shoulder. I stuck out my right hand and balled it into a fist and asked "Are we cool?"

Derek looked at me and pounded my fist and said "You know it."

"Well I am leaving in 45 minutes so you better be ready by then." I said.

"I've been ready for 15 minutes, I'm waiting on you." Derek said smiling.

# Chapter 22:

Derek and I got to Franks house right before 9 o'clock. We were the first to arrive. Frank was upstairs in the shower but he had left the front door open for us. In fact I don't think the McAdams residence was ever locked.

Earlier in the afternoon I had went with Frank to pick up the kegs, and I know what you must be thinking, how did 17 year olds get alcohol without fake ids? Well thankfully there was a nearby beer distributor owned by a wonderful Russian gentleman who did not feel the need to card minors. We tried to hide our age by letting our facial hair go unshaven. Whatever works. Frank swore that the owner was in the Russian Mafia and the store was a front for his "other" operations.

Frank had all three kegs on ice, strategically placed in three corners of the basement. The fourth corner was designated for the band. Upstairs Frank had rolled up an oriental rug and that lay on the hard wood floor. All the picture frames and valuable objects that littered the living room and dining room were carefully placed in Frank's bedroom.

"How many people are coming tonight?" Derek asked.

"I'm not sure, Frank said he was expecting like 300, but you know Frank, he's full of shit." I said.

"Yeah you mean full of himself." Derek added.

"Yeah that too." I chuckled.

My cell phone rang, it was Mike Trinoli. I answered the phone by saying "Talk to me."

Always in a hurry, Trinoli said "Hey what's up Keith, are you there yet?"

"Yeah, Derek and I just got here." I answered.

"Oh Derek's coming tonight? Cool. Is anyone else there? I'm still waiting for Eric to pick me up, he is taking forever." Trinoli said.

"No, we are the first ones here. Eric is driving? That's a first. Did you pay him?" I asked.

"Ha. Yeah right. He said that he wanted to drive tonight just in case if he changed his mind about staying over, so he could leave." Trinoli said.

"That sounds like Eric. How long are you going to be?" I asked.

"He just called me and said he was leaving. So I figure about an hour or so … just kidding probably about 10 minutes." Trinoli said.

"Okay, well we will see you then." I said.

"You better be ready for the explosion" Trinoli said before hanging up.

As I hung the phone I thought "tonight is going to be a good night". I looked at Derek and said "I'm going down stairs and tap the first keg, do you want a beer?"

Before Derek could answer Frank strolled down the stairs wearing nothing more than a towel around his waist smoking a cigarette and still wet from the shower.

"Welcome Gentlemen. I hope that you ready for tonight's festivities. Seeing you two brothers together, I must say I feel like the proud parent whose child is leaving for their first day of school. It brings a tear to my eye. Let me go get a camera." Frank joked.

"Shut up Frank." Derek said.

"Derek my boy, I am going to get you laid tonight, and I don't care what Ellen and Big Keith say. Tonight their baby becomes a man." Frank declared as he slapped his hands together, cigarette pressed between his lips

Derek's face grew a little red. And then he surprised Frank and me both by saying "Well, I better start drinking now."

"Atta' boy I knew that you had it in you. I'm not sure if you're brother told you but he is holding out for marriage." Frank continued as he looked at me with wide open eyes and a goofy smile.

"Yeah you're mother won't return any of my calls." I joked.

"Yeah well that's another thing that we have in common Sullivan because she won't return mine either." Frank said sarcastically.

"I'm sorry man, I was just kidding." I said.

Franks parents had recently divorced. Frank's mother left his father for a man she had met while on a business trip in Florida. She left Franks father a letter and said their relationship had grown stagnant and she needed a change. She packed her bags and left while Frank was at school and his father at work. Frank rarely ever mentioned his mother and with a slip of the tongue I feared I may have created an unwanted confrontation.

"Don't worry about it. I sure don't" Frank said shrugging off the ill timed remark. "Just don't be upset when you don't make any money tonight."

"What money?" Derek asked.

"You're brother, Derek, is the chairman of the party committee and contributed a major financial investment. Without him this little fiesta wouldn't have been more than but a pipe dream." Frank answered.

"How much?" Derek asked.

"Mr. Entertainment over here was short a few dollars so I spotted him. It's not a big deal. And mom and dad do not need to find out about it either." I said sternly.

"Okay, Okay don't get you're panties in a bunch, I was just asking." Derek whined.

"Oh come on now boys, there will be no arguing tonight or so help me I will turn this car right around. Now how about we take some shots?" Frank announced while raising his arms.

"Why don't you do us a favor and go put some clothes on first there Tom Cruise. This isn't Risky Business." I said.

"Yeah, you're right. I wouldn't want to embarrass either of you guys. I was thinking about going with the Hugh Hefner look tonight. You know sporting the red robe and pipe and a girl on each arm. Would that be tacky?" Frank goofed.

"Your standards of a woman would make Hugh throw out his bottle of Viagra." I joked.

"What can I say? I'm not what you would call picky. I am opportunistic and when opportunity knocks I don't stare through the peephole. I open that door and embrace the moment with open arms, and she with legs." Frank said.

"Okay guys. That's enough. Can we take some shots now?" Derek interrupted.

Frank and I could go on forever with the insults and crude remarks while other friends of ours didn't necessarily appreciate the nature of our ridicule. Frank would say if you can't joke around with your friends then who can you? I was fortunate enough to only have one class with Frank at school, not including lunch. It was history class and you already know the trouble he got me in.

We had a unique friendship. Rarely were we ever serious with one another. Most of our conversations diagnosed minor idiosyncrasies we had experienced on that of a daily basis. More often than not, time spent with Frank resulted in rib splitting humor and memorable stories.

Friendship is truly an unspoken bond between those with common interest and ideals. My mother once said that if you were able to find one true friend during the course of your life, then you should consider yourself lucky. I never looked at it that way until I got older. When you are young you surround yourself by a close knit group of friends and for a time nothing is more important than this group. The definition of a single friendship can be determined by one event. Underneath scrutiny can detect its valor and stability.

As we stood in the living room we heard the front door open and then the loud footsteps of Mike Trinoli. Trinoli was wearing a new shirt he just bought from Abercrombie and Fitch that read "All-Nighter."

The first words out of his mouth were "Like the shirt, I bought it for tonight. Where is everybody?"

"The night is young my friend, and patience is a virtue. I told everyone to get here around 9:30" Looking down to his bare wrist, pretending to be looking at his watch continued with "And seeing that it is about 9:05, I'd say you're a little early."

"Hey guys what's up?" Eric politely asked as he walked into the living room.

"Hey Eric, we were just talking about you. I hope you brought your tampons for tonight because it's about to get wild." Frank laughed.

"You're an asshole Frank, and you know that I prefer maxi-pads. They're much more comfortable" Eric replied.

"Too much information Eric, but I'm glad to see you're in a good mood. I am going to get some clothes on and then we will do some shots boys." Frank said gleefully.

The five of took a few shots of Jack Daniels. Frank stole a reserve bottle from his father's liquor cabinet. We didn't take many shots as Whiskey was much stronger that I had previously thought. We all had a good laugh when Frank said "This will put some hair on your balls, Derek."

# CHAPTER 23:

A little after 9'oclock George Marshall and his band arrived to set up in the basement. They practiced together a lot after school in George's garage and performed at the school's annual talent show and were getting ready for battle of the band's this summer. Originally they played cover songs, but recently they just started writing their own music. They had hopes of one day landing a lucrative recording contract and going on an international tour. Shortly after they arrived Frank informed them that if they gave a lousy performance that he weren't getting paid. In fact, he insisted that they should be paying him for the publicity they were going to receive.

They played great music all night and lived up to their reputation.

People began to show up in herds by 10 o'clock. The once vacant street was now lined with cars driven by underage drivers looking for a good time. Like Frank had asked I worked the front door, collecting money while Derek distributed the plastic cups. For a good half hour Frank kept us company by instructing that everyone pay $5 dollars to get inside. The price went up for uninvited guests to the tune of $10 dollars.

"If they want to get in, they'll pay it." Frank said.

The whole time I was watching the door Derek didn't leave my side unless it was to get us beer or use the bathroom. Derek provided to be great company and it was good to have a wing man as we overcharged the patrons.

About 20 minutes before midnight Frank approached us and asked us to turn in the cups. We were relieved of our duties and were no longer to be stationed at the front door. I handed him the money and he walked upstairs to lock our profits in his bedroom and it would counted later.

The turnout for the party was unreal. It was hard to imagine that so many people could fit inside a single house. The basement was packed with faithful rock listeners while those who preferred a different tune danced upstairs as the stereo systems blasted rap and hip-hop music.

While there were many new faces and some very attractive ladies at the party, I had spent most of the time talking with my brother. I opened the fridge to grab a snack and meanwhile Derek sparked up a little conversation.

"Are you nervous for college?" Derek asked.

Having a few drinks in me I was a little more open with my brother and let down my guard.

"Yeah I guess I am. I don't know what to expect. Eric and Trinoli are going to be roommates and I really couldn't live with either one of them I don't think. Eric and I would drive each other nuts and Trinoli is too wild. I guess I am a little anxious about not knowing my roommate." I confessed.

"Yeah I can imagine" Derek paused "I'm sorry that you didn't get in to Penn State." Derek said.

"Thanks D. That means a lot to me. But I don't think Montgomery is going to be so bad. I hear that it's second largest party school in the state plus I already know the major I'm going to take so I guess I am excited." I said.

"Do you think you'll try out for the basketball team?" Derek asked.

"You know what Derek, I haven't really thought about that yet. Maybe. I don't know. I don't know if I want to go through that bullshit again. Sports are politics. I could always join a fraternity or something." I said, now thinking about the future.

"I don't know about that Keith. I heard that they make you do some really crazy things when you are pledging. You heard what cousin Gary said last Christmas. He said that his roommate Luke joined a fraternity and they made him drink piss." Derek said.

"No, they didn't make him drink piss. He had to roll around in cold spaghetti that was supposedly peed on." I said correcting him. As if rolling around in urine was classier than drinking it.

"Well either way that's still really gross. Gary also said that Luke had to get naked a lot and run around campus." Derek continued on with the negative preconceived connotations of Greek Life.

"Well whatever. I didn't say that I was definitely going to do it. It was just a thought. It's just an option." I said.

"There are a lot of people here Keith. I can't believe it's this packed." Derek said changing the subject.

"Yeah I know. I have to admit it. That bastard Frank came through tonight." I agreed.

As we walked into the living room and watched the drunks dance, Derek and I could not help but notice Wendi Miller. Wendi was in my grade and was a co-captain of the field hockey team. She had light brown hair and green eyes and a pretty smile. Wendi was looking pretty good in her designer tank top and skirt and how her eyes were glued to Derek. For the majority of her time at school she went steady with Brian Oliver who was the goalie for the soccer team. They had recently broken up, which is probably the reason why she was at Frank's party. Rumor had it that Brian was caught cheating on her with her friend Stephanie Lewis from the field hockey team.

As her and her friends danced in the living room she started to continually smile at Derek. This direct acknowledgement of my little brother acted as an invitation to come join her. Like his older brother Derek wasn't aggressive when it came to women. In fact he was quite shy when it came to matters of the opposite sex. Tonight, however, he was a little buzzed and feeling courageous.

"I'm going to go dance with her!" Derek proclaimed to me quite boldly.

"Oh yeah? Go do it Romeo." I jokingly said, as I did not believe Derek would follow through on his words.

Much to my surprise Derek carefully approached Wendi Miller and the two started to dance. I could not believe my eyes as I watched my little brother break out of his shell.

A few moments later Frank walked over to me and put his left hand around my shoulder spilling a little bit of beer on my shirt. "They grow up so fast." He amusingly said before taking a puff of a freshly sparked joint. He again offered me to join.

"You never quit do you?" I said to Frank.

"Nope. It's not in my nature to quit. So, what do you say?" Frank said

Before I could turn down Frank's offer I was saved by Mike Trinoli who screamed to me "You're brother's a stud." Frank and I looked over and before our eyes we saw Derek and Wendi kissing on the dance floor.

"I knew he had it in him, he certainly doesn't get it from you. It must be from Keith Senior. Only a stud like your dad could land a sophisticated lady like Ellen." Frank said.

"Don't push your luck McAdams." I said trying to appear irritated before a smile escaped on my face.

Soon thereafter, Derek stumbled on over with a large silly grin on his face. "Hey guys," he yelled. "Frank, could you do me a favor? Is there a room upstairs that Wendi and I can use?"

"What happened to my brother?" I said jokingly. "This isn't the same person I've come to know, did Frank slip something into your drink?"

"Come on Keith, don't you have any faith in me? I'm saving that for later tonight." Frank said. Returning his attention to Derek's question, "Yes, I have a spare bedroom upstairs that you and little miss lovely may use, but you're going to have to let me watch."

"Okay, but I don't know if Wendi will be cool with that. But I guess I can ask." Derek said with a confused look on his face.

"Just kidding Casanova, I'm just kidding. But I do believe that you need another shot of Jack Daniels. Oh and this." Frank said while putting his hand in his pocket and then handing a condom to Derek. Still looking puzzled Derek took the condom from Frank.

"Don't worry about me. I have plenty more. Now come on, let's go do some shots." Frank said.

As Frank walked away with Trinoli to the kitchen and pulled out the now half filled bottle of Jack Daniels from one of the cabinets, Derek looked at me and said "I've never had sex before Keith."

"Neither have I." I said

"Really?" Derek asked sounding surprised.

"Of course I have. But it's really not that big of deal. Everyone seems to make such a big deal about it. It's only sex." I replied.

"What if we don't have sex? What if she doesn't want to? What if I don't want to?" Derek nervously asked. His confidence now dissipated after the brief interaction with Frank.

"You don't have to have sex tonight. It's not the end of the world Derek. And don't listen to Frank. He will sleep with anything with teeth. It's okay to have self respect. You're only 16 and there will be plenty of other girls to have sex with. Besides Wendi just got out of a long relationship and I don't think she is that type of girl." I said.

"Come on girls, I am waiting." Frank shouted over to me and my brother.

Before Derek could walk over and join our gracious host, I grabbed his arm and said "Hey, take it easy on the liquor, okay?"

"I will *DAD*. Just one more shot, I'm feeling good over here!" Derek said.

As Derek walked over to engage in another round of spirits, he stumbled a little bit. He was already fairly drunk and didn't really need any more alcohol. I wasn't going to be too over protective. The night was young and, as he so eloquently stated earlier, he was old enough to take care of himself.

While Frank, Derek and Trinoli took shots I walked over to Wendi Miller and said with a smile "I never knew that you liked younger guys." Her face grew a little blush and in her cutest voice she said "Shut up, Keith!"

"It's okay. When guys date younger girls they are made fun of but when girls rock the cradle everything is flowers and roses. I like double standards." I said jokingly.

"I have always thought that you're brother was SO cute. He has the prettiest blue eyes that I have ever seen." She said bashfully.

"Yeah. Well you take good care of him." I said.

"Oh, I will." She said convincingly.

I couldn't help but feel a little envious of Derek. I always had a small crush on Wendi, but she was always in a relationship.

I walked back over to the guys as they were finishing a round of shots. "Your brother is a machine Sullivan. He just pounded three shots." Trinoli said loudly.

"Damn it guys that's enough. Don't give him any more shots. I mean it! He is done." I demanded.

"Oh come on Keith. I am fine. I can hang with the big boys I'm not a little girl like you." Derek said. His words were now beginning to slur a little bit and his eyes were a little cloudy.

"Ok Romeo. Juliet is waiting for you. Why don't you go upstairs now and dazzle her with your charm and hope she doesn't laugh when you take your pants off." I responded to his insult.

Derek gave me a goofy smile and said "Don't be jealous." He gave my face a subtle smack quickly before he walked away.

As he and Wendi subtly headed upstairs I returned my attention back to Trinoli and Frank as I was a little upset that they were feeding my 16 year old brother liquor.

"Oh lighten up Sullivan. Your brother is just having a good time. Let him enjoy himself." Frank argued.

"Hey, if you don't mind him throwing up all over your house than be my guest and give Derek more shots." I said.

Quickly changing the conversation Frank looked over at Trinoli and asked "Where is Erica, did she get a stain on her blouse?

Trinoli laughed at Frank's comments and said "No, he is down stairs with Bryan Goldman listening to the band. You know he is in that type of music."

"That's right, I almost forgot about the band." I said.

"I'm going to go listen for a little bit, I'll check you guys later."

# CHAPTER 24:

As I entered Frank's large unfinished basement I was quickly astonished at the amount of people that filled the room. It was the first time during the night that I had made it down there. I walked over to the keg to refill my beer and two kegs were already kicked and it was only 12:30. I walked over to Eric and Bryan Goldman and asked how the band was.

Eric who was visibly drunk was immensely enjoying himself nodded his head and said "They're good. Yeah they are real good."

Bryan Goldman quickly agreed with Eric by saying "They are amazing," in his usually annoying voice.

Eric played guitar and was extremely talented. The guy could listen to a song on the radio and within a few minutes start strumming along with the song. He wrote and played his own music and we persistently tried to convince him to join a band. Eric had the fear of playing in front of a live audience. It was quite frustrating as a fan of his music because he truly was a gifted musician.

Bryan Goldman had a few classes with us and it was rumored, by us, that he had a serious man crush on Eric. Bryan was an aspiring musician and constantly asked Eric to join him in "Jam Sessions." While Eric was particularly annoyed by Bryan, he didn't know how to tell him NO, so he just dealt with him.

After asking Eric a few questions, only to be interrupted by Bryan, I decided to give up. I quickly drank from my cup so I could excuse myself from their remarkable conversation.

As I walked back over to the keg I saw a large individual filling their cup. It was someone who I was very familiar with and hadn't seen in a couple years. Steven Thompson, was two grades above me, was a dominating left handed baseball player. In his junior year alone, the 6'5 flame thrower brought Adams to the brink of the public league championship with a blistering fast ball consistently clocked in the high 80's, which was complimented by a curve ball that danced in and out of the strike zone. Unfortunately his pitching arsenal and public league record 422 foot homerun wasn't enough and Adams would fall short 2-1 to Roosevelt High School.

Going into his senior year Thompson was the cities highest rated High School Baseball Player and a highly sought after college recruit. When he wasn't pitch he was on first base. He was too athletic and his bat to deadly to be sitting on the bench in between starts. Thompson would fail to reach academic eligibility the quarter before his senior season. No amount of sweet talking or "recommendations" from Principal Cald or Coach O'Brien could get his teachers to raise his grade point average. "Only if he would have shown up to class they would say." Thompson fell in with the wrong crowd skipping class and getting high was their alternative to learning.

In an attempt to still be recruited into the Major Leagues he joined the American Legion baseball program and was steadily making a name for himself as his terrific play brought out professional recruiters to his games. One Saturday morning as the stands packed with fans and scouts, Thompson wanted their attention and intended to do so by increasing the velocity of his fastball.

Midway through the fifth inning of a no-hitter Thompson would dislocate his elbow throwing his untouchable fastball. Tearing ligaments in his left arm he would eventually require the revered Tommy Johns surgery. His father's health care plan no longer covered Thompson since he was over the age of 18 and not enrolled in college. With the rise of medical cost and surgery Steve Thompson had to settle for an inadequate doctor and the surgery was not a success. Although he rehabbed relentlessly, the setback would prove too costly. Thompson would spend a year and a half trying to repair the arm and continue his quest for a shot at professional baseball. However, the injury deteriorated his velocity and his optimism. Discouraged, he would hang up his cleats and give up on his dream of being a professional ball player.

As I waited for him to finish filling his beer, he looked up at me and handed me the tap and said enthusiastically "Hey what's up Sullivan?"

I was a little surprised that he remembered me. He was a very popular student in his day at John Adams and we really weren't what you would call friends.

"Hey. Nothing much Steve, how have you been?" I said as we then shook hands.

"I'm doing great man. Are you ready for graduation?" He asked.

"Yeah I guess so. I mean I can't wait to get out of Adams. But it's whatever. How long have you been here for?" I said.

"My girlfriend and I just got here. Her sister goes to Saint Mary's and told us about the party. She wanted to stop by for a little bit before we went bar hopping, but we probably are just going to stay here now."

"That's cool man." Not knowing what else to say as there was a brief pause "You want to take a couple shots? This is my friend's house and we have some whiskey upstairs." I asked.

"Yeah sure, I'm just going to go tell my girlfriend real quick, she'll get nervous." Thompson said.

The big fellow returned and we walked upstairs and entered the kitchen. I remembered where Frank had stashed the bottle of whiskey and I took out two clean shot glasses for Steve and myself. I poured the shots. We said cheers, clanked our glasses and took the shots. All and all we took 3 shots and I was feeling good, really good. I did not drink much up until this point. I was trying to pace myself as I had a little more stake in the party than I would normally.

"Can you smoke in here?" Thompson asked.

"No. Frank doesn't want anyone smoking inside, but you can go out on the back patio." I answered.

"Want a cigarette?' Thompson then asked.

"Sure." I said, against my better judgment. I didn't normally smoke cigarettes. I was what you call a social smoker. When I was drinking, I enjoyed tobacco for it masked the taste of alcohol.

Steve and I walked outside and engaged in a smoke and began to talk about Adams and the sports in which we participated. I told him what had happened during the basketball season and he then began to tell me about the trials and tribulations he faced on the baseball diamond. He spoke of his injury and the major disappointment he had faced. It was quite strange having a heart to heart with someone I barely knew.

Steve Thompson looked at me with a tragic sense of failed accomplishment and said "When the first Doctor told me I wasn't going to able to play baseball again at the same level I was used to playing and that my pitching career was over. I thought my life was over. And for a time it was. I wanted to kill myself man. I put a single bullet in my father's .45, put the barrel in my mouth and had the finger on the trigger. I just couldn't pull the trigger. I started to cry. All I ever wanted to do was be a ball player, there wasn't any alternative."

I was taken back from the candor and the sincerity of his words as he described his failure. I wasn't quite sure how to approach the conversation as he was in such a vulnerable state.

Feeling slightly more intoxicated I felt the need to be supportive and asked "How is everything now?"

"I'm not going to lie; it's been difficult, really difficult. I could have easily given up. I wanted too, who wouldn't. I thought I had the easy road to success but I have found out that adversity really tests a person's character. I guess I was lucky though. I was recommended to a really good physical therapist. She turned my life around." He said.

"Really? Well that's great." I said.

"Besides the fact that she was the most beautiful woman I had ever met she was just so positive and influential during my recovery. At first I really didn't respond to her I was too depressed. I was never gonna play ball again. I wasn't going to go to college. I didn't have a future." He added.

"The second week into rehab she yelled at me and said if I didn't get my act together to look for another PT. And I'll never forget what she said." He paused for a second as if he were replaying her words in his head.

"She looked at me with this passion and fire in her eyes and said: "What you had is lost. It's gone, it's over. What you have and what you need is what is real. You have your youth and you need to move on with your life and rehabilitate your arm." I said to her that "I'm sorry but that's not enough for me, it's not what I want. She said "it's going to have to be."

Steve continued "She asked me "What are you going to give up, are you going to quit? You don't look like a quitter to me. You have a lot of potential. Anyone can quit. Quitting is the easy way out and I'm not going to let you quit. It takes courage to face your fear and keep going. No matter what happens you always keep moving."

"And that's what I did, after her little "pep talk." I had to really take a look at the path I had to take. It became my motivation. It turned my life around." Steve Thompson added. "I'm finally done rehabilitating my arm, it has been a long two years, but now I can go onto the next challenge."

"That's awesome man, what are you doing now?" I asked.

"Well I am about to start going to school to be a personal trainer. It's a year program and afterwards I want to start my own business. I can train clients from their homes or at a gym." Thompson said proudly.

"That's awesome." I said.

"Yeah, I'm excited about it. It's going to be tough but I'll do it. I'm up for it" Karl went on.

"Alright, well I'm gonna go back in and check on the old ball and chain but it was really good talking to you. Thanks for the shots." Karl said. He forgot to add that the ball and chain he aforementioned was the personal trainer who was so instrumental in his rehabilitation.

After we shook hands Steve removed his cell phone from his pants pocket and said "Why don't you give your cell phone number. Just in case if you ever need a personal trainer."

A few years after this exchange I would run into Steve at Wall-Mart, and he was well on his way to establishing the business that he had mentioned to me at Frank's party. He even began to instruct other trainers.

It strange how some friendships seem to start from a candid conversation with a relative stranger.

We exchanged numbers and then reentered the party. As we parted ways I had seen Frank standing in the kitchen observing the party. Frank walked over and sarcastically said "Where's your new friend going?"

"What are you jealous or something?" I asked jokingly.

"A little bit, yes." Frank replied.

"Where have you been, I haven't seen you in a while?" I asked.

"Well I just so happened to bump into Jenny McNamara and she was kind enough to accompany me upstairs and we participated in some activities we learned in health class." Frank said.

Before I could insult him, Frank stuck his hand in his pocket and pulled out a cleanly stacked wad of cash, quickly eyed it, and handed it to me. "We grossed in just over $1,000 for tonight." Frank said.

"1,000 bucks, are you serious?!" I asked emphatically.

"Well if you think about, there was over 200 people, 5 dollars a cup. You do the math. It's about right. I told George Marshall I'd give $150 for his band playing on such short notice but I didn't take it out of your cut. We made our money back and then some. Everyone is having a good time. I'd say it was a success." Frank added.

Frank had given me back $515 on my $150 "investment," as he called it. It was a nice profit indeed $465. It was just after quarter of 1 and the party was still going strong, that is, until the final keg ran out of beer. Many of the partiers began to slowly disperse and it was a good thing. Frank and I had discussed going to a nearby 24 hour diner once everyone had left.

Walking down the stairs was Wendi Miller who had a look of disappointment on her face. She walked over towards Frank to me and I asked her "What's wrong?"

She let out a sigh and said, "You're Brother passed out on me while we were… kissing …"

Before she could finish Frank quickly interrupted. He couldn't let the opportunity slip by without making one of his usual juvenile annotations. "Isn't the guy supposed to fall asleep, afterwards?" He asked.

Wendi offered Frank one of the fiercest looks I had ever seen and retorted "I'm not that type of girl, jerk, we were only kissing."

Wendi returned her attention to me and then asked timidly. "My friend's want to leave and I wanted to say goodbye but. Do you think that you could, that you could give me Derek's number?"

"Yeah, sure." I said. I recited the number to the eager Wendi as she programmed Derek's number into her cell phone.

"Thanks guys. Tell Derek that I'll call him tomorrow, bye!" She said with a smile and walked away with her friends.

"You think if they get married that you'll be the best man?" Frank asked.

"Shut up." I replied.

"Well I'm throwing the bachelor party," Frank said. "Well it's time to kick all these free loaders out, maestro if you will?"

"What?" I asked, not fully understanding what Frank meant.

"Yeah, you're right. If you want something done right you've got to do it yourself." Frank said.

It was now almost quarter of two. Frank walked over to the stereo and turned the volume down. He began to shout "Can I have everyone's attention! It is now closing time and the bar is now closed. You don't have to go home but you need to get the hell out of here. Management thanks you for patronage and cooperation, so if you would please finish your drinks and then head towards the exit."

Frank and I then walked downstairs and Frank gave a similar speech. George Marshall's band had already stopped playing and was in the midst of packing up their equipment. All three kegs were kicked and the basement appeared to be in pretty good shape seeing as the large concrete slab had no carpeting or flooring and stored nothing of real worth besides an old beat up pool table and unused exercise equipment.

As many of its inhabitants began to trudge up the stairs, an unfamiliar looking girl and her friend walked over to Frank and me. She was dressed as if the party were a photo shoot for maxim magazine along with her friend. Joanne and Kerri were old friends of Frank from Archbishops Donovan's sister school St. Mary's catholic school for girls. Despite their rich morals and religious upbringing, catholic girls had the reputation for being somewhat promiscuous, at least the ones I knew.

Joanne said to Frank as she batted her eyelashes "This was such an awesome party, the band was great and there was SO many people, I can't believe it …But, we were kind of hoping that, not everyone had to leave." She went on to say.

"Well as a matter of fact, my colleague and I were just discussing the possibility of an after party." Frank said.

"Well" Joanne said as she placed her hand on Frank's chest and slowly ran her until ending slightly below his belt, "I hope that we make the list."

"I might have to pull some strings, but I'll see what I can do." Frank said with smile.

"Good." Joanne said in her sexiest voice as she grabbed Frank's crotch. The two girls turned and walked away as they softly giggled to one another.

"I'll tell ya something Sullivan. They just don't make 'em like that in public school." Frank said as he adjusted his pants. Usually at this juncture Frank would offer an outrageous anecdote directly related to the previous events. At the present time he was more concerned with clearing the masses from his father's house. But I'm quite sure his eagerness to clear out the basement was so that he could attend to more personal matters.

"Yeah, I'll say." I said a little surprise at what had just transpired. "Are you cool down here? I'm going to go check on Derek real quick."

"Yeah I'm good." Frank answered "But don't keep me waiting, I don't look nearly as intimidating without you standing next to me."

"Well Eric is down here, you'll be fine." I said jokingly, knowing the statement would cause slight rue. Frank and Eric were known to disagree on many subjects and Frank had repeatedly questioned Eric's intestinal fortitude. I guess you could say that they were friends by association, and the two would rarely be alone together for a long duration without arguing.

"That's the most comforting you said all night." Frank said before he walked away towards George Marshall to discuss the night and pay him for his services.

As I made my way towards the stairwell I felt someone grab my left arm, it was my new found friend Kerri. "I hope you're not leaving." She said coyly.

"Uh. No. I'm just going upstairs for a minute." I said

"Okay, well I better see you back down here in five minutes then." She said, gently sliding her hand down my arm as she briefly held my hand.

"I'll be back." I said giving my worst impersonation of Arnold Schwarzenegger from the Terminator. "Smooth," I thought as I ascended the stairs. It was a good thing Frank wasn't around. I'd never hear the end of it. I wasn't known to be the suave when it came to female interaction. I normally played the quiet one. Girls often thought that I was shy. I just didn't want to make a fool of myself and say something stupid. Not everyone really understood my dry sense of humor.

As I made it to the living room I noticed two guys arguing with each other, almost coming to blows. The night was had been far too perfect for something like this happen at the conclusion of the party. Apparently it was inevitable. I quickly approached the situation so that I could see what the problem was. Like many drunk altercations this one centered on a female counterpart. I was able to mediate the two got them to leave without dropping their gloves. The problem was solved and I was able to continue upstairs to check out my love sick brother.

When I got to the bedroom Derek and Wendi had once vacated, I found the room empty and with a foul aroma. I flipped on the light switched and noticed a little vomit at the foot of the bed and on the floor underneath. I walked to the hallway bathroom that was directly across from the bedroom and found the door locked. I knocked heavily on the door and called Derek's name aloud, hoping that he was not passed out. After I said his name a few times I heard some movement in the bathroom. A moment later Derek forced out the words "I'll be right out." Derek was lying on the bathroom floor praying to the porcelain gods.

"Derek, open the door now." I demanded. "I told you not to drink so damn much. Open the door."

Derek was coherent and able to pick himself off the floor and unlock the bathroom door before falling back onto the cold tiles. I opened the door to find him without his shirt on and the faucet running. When I stepped inside he asked "Did Wendi leave?"

"Yes. She did but not before I gave her your phone number." I said, now starting to laugh at my incapacitated brother. "Is that a hickey on your neck?" I asked as I noticed the golf ball sized bruise on his neck.

"Where?" Derek asked in excitement as he attempted to stand, he hit the back of his head on the sink.

"You're a mess." I said before I grabbed him as he began to stumble. I forced his head under the running water and requested that he drink some water in attempt so that he could sober up. "And put your shirt back on you're not impressing anybody."

I went back to the spare bedroom and removed the soiled sheets. I balled them up and walked them back into the bathroom and threw them into the tub. "I'll take care of this later." I thought. I was more concerned about Derek than Franks dirty bed sheets. Frank may have felt otherwise but who's to say. When I made sure Derek had drank enough water I escorted back into the bedroom and laid him down.

I returned back down stairs with the living to find Frank and Trinoli standing with Joanne and Kerri. Frank had managed to round up the rest of the stragglers from the basement as about 25-30 partiers still conversed in the living room.

Meanwhile Trinoli and Kerri were engaged in an in-depth conversation. It wouldn't be the first time Trinoli would steal away a prospective female companion. It wasn't his fault; he had a genuine quality that girls adored and was well renowned for his sincere demeanor and personality. Girls always said they loved his curiosity and smile. I couldn't blame him, Kerri was very attractive and I had not yet expressed any interest. I didn't make a big fuss about it, although I was a little upset as she was quite attractive.

Frank had spoken with about 10-15 of his friends during the party and expressed his intentions of having a remainder of them stay for an after party. I was more interested in going out to Andonio's 24 hour diner and grabbing their signature cheeseburger and french-fries but for now it didn't look like it was going to happen.

# CHAPTER 25:

With the party now dwindled to just a few close friends, we began to recap the night.

It sure did go fast, and it was hard to believe that the highly anticipated night was coming to a close. As we sat in Franks living room discussing transpired events, Joanne and Kerri felt that they needed a little pick me up. They secretly dispersed into the kitchen with Frank as they broke out a small saran wrap bag filled with cocaine.

"I'm sorry girls, I don't party like that." Frank said as his loud voice could be overheard in the living room.

I guess I was fortunate growing up that I was never really exposed to drugs or violence like the many other kids my age that lived in the city. My parents weren't divorced and I had positive role models in my life to steer me away from making wrong decisions and falling in with the wrong crowd. It seems more evident to me now that the people we associate with can directly impact the actions we take. Many of my friends were student athletes and involved with other school related events. Getting out of school at 2:15 every day, left student's with hours to participate in unsupervised extra-curricular activities. Not every student is so fortunate to find an alcove in after school programming that provided them with what athletics did for me.

"What are you a faggot?" Joanne rudely yelled.

"Well, not so much a faggot as that I just don't appreciate drug use in my father's house or your overall tone for that matter. But you can do me a favor and you can get the hell out of my house." Frank snapped back with a sarcastic smile.

"Fine! Let's go Kerri. I knew that you guys were a bunch of loser's anyway." Joanne snapped as she grabbed her things and stormed out of the kitchen.

Kerri appeared reluctant to leave and apologized to Frank before she left. She exited a little more quietly than her fuming friend. Frank walked back into the living room with a look of disdain on his face and said "Well, where were we?"

Frank periodically dissected his "Time in Catholicism," as he would call it. He often quoted the now late, great George Carlin and say that "I was a catholic until I reached the age of reason." He said that he found it comical that the religion allowed sinners to be resolved of their sins every Sunday, no matter how appalling or inconceivable the offense they committed. On a weekly basis all was forgiven by a man, not god himself. However, reciting the occasional Hail Mary would be required for their penance.

When I would ask Frank about his time in the confessional, he would say that he wasn't a hypocrite and never asked for forgiveness of his sins because there was nothing that he regretted.

He particularly found it ridiculous that his school teachers and priests condemned their students for masturbating but the church covered up any allegations of sexual abuse against children and ignored growing complaints of molestation.

Shortly thereafter the Joanne's outburst most of the remaining guest's parted ways and the once filled house was left with those who started the night with shot of Jack Daniels: Frank, Trinoli, Eric and myself, along with Derek upstairs sleeping.

"How about we go to the diner?" I suggested, still experiencing that strong craving for a late night fix.

As the other guys concurred, I grew eager as we were about to embark to a fine dining establishment and indulge in a highly anticipated after hours meal. Before we could get our act in gear the doorbell rang and in entered our late night misfortunes.

Justin Bradley was at Frank's front door claiming he had left his cell phone somewhere in the house and was disinclined to leave without it, however, Frank was reluctant to let the intoxicated Justin back into the house.

At the same moment Derek stumbled down the stairs and with a silly grin on his face as he proclaimed. "Wendi just called me to make sure that I was okay and we talked for five minutes. She's so great."

"Back from the dead, I thought we lost you there buddy." Trinoli said.

"Yeah I'm back. I'm sorry about your bed Frank, I'll clean it tomorrow." Derek continued.

"Yeah, Frank I forgot to tell you." I interjected.

"Forgot to tell me what?" Frank asked.

"Derek kind of regurgitated in the spare bedroom, but I'll clean the sheets." I said cautiously.

"Oh don't' worry about it, I never sleep in that bed, I don't care." Frank said with a smile.

Justin, whose eyes were completely glazed over, stumbled onto the sofa and asked "Hey, could one of you guys call my cell phone."

"What's your number?" Eric asked as he pulled out his phone and flipped open its cover.

"2 6 7 4 8 9 5 1 2 5" Justin recited his cell phone number painfully slow.

Eric dialed the numbers and we waited for a moment in anticipation to see if we could hear the phone ring. A few seconds later a faint vibration could be heard. Justin stood up and placed his right hand in his back left pocket and pulled out the hidden cell phone. Too drunk to be embarrassed Justin stated "Oh, I must have had it in the wrong pocket."

"You're an idiot." Frank laughed.

Uneasy about Justin's physical condition Eric asked "Are you sure you're going to be able to drive home."

"I'll be fine man. I live like five seconds away." Justin answered as he stumbled for the door.

"Hey, could you drive me somewhere?" Derek asked Justin.

"You're not going anywhere." I said to Derek.

Ignoring my comments Derek continued "Could you Justin, it's on the way?"

"Yeah sure bro man. Where too?" Justin asked.

"I'm going to Wendi Millers house." Derek announced in a loud voice.

"Did she ask you to come over?" I asked.

"No" Derek replied, "But I figured that I would surprise her."

"I don't think that's such a good idea buddy. Going to a girl's house unannounced late at night is usually considered. Just follow standard operating procedures when obtaining a girls phone number and call her in three days." Frank added, being a much needed voice of reason.

"Yeah, it's a bad idea Derek. Why don't you go to the diner with us?" Trinoli said.

"I'm not hungry. I want to go see Wendi." Derek said, nearly stomping his feet like a 5 year old.

"Hey moron, do you think Wendi is going to appreciate you stumbling on her front lawn. What are you intending to do? Throw rocks at her window? Sing love songs to her? You don't even know where she lives." I said, now losing my patience.

"I know where she lives man. She is only just a few blocks down from me. My sister used to be friends with her sister" Justin stated.

"Okay, let's go." Derek eagerly said as he headed for the doorway.

Frank stepped in front of Derek and looked at Justin and said "Justin I think it's better if you leave, NOW!" Justin exited the front door and Derek then took out some frustration as he yelled at Frank and me.

Frank then grabbed Derek by the collar and yelled "Hey, your brother is a good friend of mine, actually I consider him like a brother. So guess what? That makes you family, and if your brother doesn't want you to go then I don't want you to go and that means you're not going. So calm down, sober up and have a good time before I tie you up and throw you in a closet for the rest of the night."

"Hey, alright, okay." Derek stammered. "No need to get so angry."

After the little riff the rest of the guys felt that they no longer wanted to go the diner and to just stay put. Derek fell back asleep on a couch in the living room and so I picked him up and for the second time put him to sleep upstairs. Frank had some frozen pizza in the fridge and he threw them in the oven and we patiently waited for the hot snack. The fun would not be over, however, as our night was just about to get started.

A little while after his departure Justin would return bloodied and disoriented. He loudly pounded on Frank's front door. He began to scream open up before Frank could answer. Justin had pieces of glass on his clothing and cuts on his face. His shirt was torn and he nearly fainted before he could sit down.

"What the hell happened, Justin?!" we all asked.

A little more than ¾ of a mile into the drive Justin drove off of Mason Hill Road into a ditch and collided with a tree. His car was totaled. It was a miracle he even survived.

"Somebody ran me off the road, man." Justin stammered as he began to fall asleep.

"Where?" Frank asked. "Where were you? Wake up!" Frank screamed.

"Relax man … it was right down the road." Justin said laughingly, "My parents are going to kill me. They just gave me that car."

Frank walked into the kitchen and quickly filled a glass of water from the faucet he walked back into the living room and threw the cold contents onto Justin's face. "Listen you fucking idiot, this is not a joke. Why didn't you call one of us? Did you call the police?" Frank asked with a level of seriousness I have never heard in his voice.

"I don't have you're guys numbers and besides my cell phone broke. I couldn't call anybody." Justin answered.

"Well what about the car that ran you off the road. Did they stop and see if you were alright?" Trinoli asked.

"Um… No… I don't think they saw it…No one stopped. I didn't see anyone. I just got out of the car and ran here." Justin stuttered.

"Do you realize the shit I will be in if the cops find out I had kegs here. I distributed alcohol to minors. My dad will get sued. Then he will kill me. He will send me to some boot camp in the middle of the god damn dessert. Are you sure no one called the police." Frank asked demandingly.

"I told you I don't know. Why don't you go down there and see." Justin suggested.

"That's exactly what I'll do." Frank said.

"Are you sure that's such a good idea Frank." I interrupted. "What if c ops are there? We're drunk. If they stop us we could …?" Before I could finish Frank would calmly say "Hey, I'll drive, I barely had anything to drink other than a few shots. I'm fine to drive. If we see red and blue flashing lights then we're just going to nonchalantly drive on by roll down the windows and asked what the hell happened. Everybody loves a good accident. They can't arrest us for looking or being nosey, so get your shit together and let's go."

"I'm not going to go." Eric stated.

"Okay then Eric, you stay here and make sure Justin doesn't fall asleep, there is a good chance he has a concussion" Frank said

"Well how do I do that?" Eric inquired.

"I don't know Eric be creative. Just make sure that you don't let him sleep until we get back." Frank insisted.

Frank, Trinoli and I got into Franks car and we drove down to Mason Hill road. I knew Frank was more intoxicated than he led us to believe but there was no way of convincing him to stay put and I wasn't about to let him drive alone.

As we approached the disabled vehicle Frank slowed down. Police had yet to arrive at the scene and we were in the clear for the moment. We parked a few yards behind the wreck so that we could examine the crash. What we were about to see was unexpected and quite frightening. Justin's car had to be speeding down the windy road. The car resembled an accordion, with the windshield completely shattered, the left turn signal flashing, smoke sputtering from the exhaust pipe because somehow the engine was still running. The scene smelled of burnt rubber and melting engine belts.

The car was tightly pressed against a small unforgiving tree. It was amazing how the impact of the fast moving heavy piece of machinery caused no significant damage to this little tree. It hardly rocked the earth's foundation. Deeper analysis of the wreck would prove more startling. A thick low hanging branch was the culprit for the shattered windshield. The branch extended through the passenger side seat and penetrated right through. The very tip of the branch rested a few inches above the back seat. The vision left me speechless.

It was apparently obvious to me that if someone was riding with Justin they would have not survived. The impact with the tree limb would have impaled the passenger quite possibly severing them in half. If it weren't for us Derek would have been in the car and I would have lost my little brother. Pardon the morbidity of this description as I'm just trying to really paint the severity of the circumstances.

The sound of sirens began to groan in the distance as we were temporarily paralyzed by the grim reality of the accident.

"Come on guys we need to leave now," Trinoli said snapping us out of the momentary daze. "We need to move."

We ran to Frank's car and off we went, making a right down the first available street. To be extra cautious Frank drove with his headlights off. Not a single word was said as Frank navigated through the dark streets back to his house. The gravity of the situation was overwhelming. The vision of the accident continued to replay in my thoughts and to this day I can picture it as though I was still standing there. I can even smell that terrible burnt rubber smell.

It is truly amazing that Justin survived the crash. Why is it that a drunk driver survives on a more consistent basis as than the sober responsible driver they collide with? I once heard someone say that the reason could be is that alcohol consumption slows down the heart rate and causes muscles to grow numb, therefore driving under the influence causes drivers to be less tense during the moments before impact. It is not to my knowledge that there have been any studies that link muscle tenseness with the disparity of injuries resulting from a car crash but I guess that it is possible that you can relate the two.

When we got back to Frank's house Eric immediately opened the front door and had a panicked look on his face.

"I told you to not let Justin fall asleep you can't leave him alone for a second Eric." Frank said as he got out of the car.

"Well we have a problem Frank because he fell asleep and I can't wake him up. I didn't know what do you guys, so I ..." Eric stammered.

"So you..?" I asked.

"...I um. I called for an ambulance." Eric answered.

"You did what? Why would you do that Eric? Why didn't you call us first?" Frank screamed.

"He wouldn't wake up. I got nervous Frank. I don't know CPR. I'm not a doctor. I didn't want to get involved. I don't know this kid. I just wanted to go home but I don't this on my conscience. I can't be held responsible if he dies. I had to call them you guys. He needs medical attention. He needed my help, and this was the only way I knew how." Eric responded.

"Jesus Christ, Eric ... There are three kegs in the basement. There are cups and cigarette butts all over the floor. They're going to know there was a party here." Frank said as he put his hands on his head.

"Not if we stop arguing and start cleaning." Trinoli said.

"The upstairs doesn't look too bad. I already started throwing out cups." Eric said.

"Well let's not just stand here with our thumbs up our butts. We don't have much time here." I added.

We quickly worked together in an attempt to clean a house once filled with upwards of 220 underage teenagers in a matter of minutes. We were hoping that the police lived up their reputation and responded in their normal manner to Eric's call for help. Trinoli and Eric stayed up stairs while Frank and I tackled the basement. The basement reeked of the spilled beer and a legion of cigarette butts littered the cement floor along with white plastic cups.

"I'll clean the floor Keith, you make those kegs disappear." Frank said as he held a push broom in his hands.

Easier said than done I thought. I could only manage to grab two of the three empty kegs in my hands. I ran up the basements steps and quickly exited through the sliding glass doors in the kitchen and entered the backyard. I had forgotten to turn on the lights, but no matter, I had to find a suitable hiding spot. I ran to end of the property line and underneath a glorious set of bushes I laid down the two kegs. The spot looked good enough for me and I ran back inside for the remaining keg.

For the second time tonight I heard the sound of sirens, this time they were loud and distinct. Sirens that were once previously thought to be responding to Justin's car crash were in response to Eric's 911 call. The sound that had returned our sobriety had now brought with it fear. I ran back inside and slammed the sliding door behind me and yelled "They are here!"

"Oh shit" Eric said "I'm still too drunk. I can't be here for this. I'm just going to go upstairs and pretend I'm asleep. I can't get in trouble. I can't."

"But you're the one who called them in the first place Eric you can't just bail on us on now. We wouldn't be in this mess if it wasn't for you." Trinoli bellowed, expressing his frustration.

"I didn't give them my name Mike. It's not my fault he crashed. You guys left me here with him so you could go and check out the accident. I didn't know what to do." Eric replied.

The basement door opened and Frank walked into the living room. A cigarette pressed in his lips a sense of calmness entered with him. "Go upstairs Eric. I'll tell them that I called. This is my house I'll take responsibility for it." Frank looked at Trinoli and me and said "If you guys want to go upstairs to, I'll understand. There is no reason for us all to get in trouble here."

I was almost relieved by his cool demeanor. EMS attendants were about to pound on his door and he was hardly unnerved. The situation had really shown Franks true colors.

"No Frank. We went in on this together, I'm sticking around." I proclaimed.

"Yeah, I'm cool dude." Trinoli added.

Eric turned his head and proceeded to head up the stairs. I can understand Eric's stance as it was a difficult situation to be in. In hind sight he made the right decision to call for emergency help but we couldn't help but be angry for him wanting to not be present when they arrived. He was never one for confrontation and did what he could to avoid them. Whenever any of us argued and asked him for any support or confirmation on a matter, he would say "I'm not getting involved." This time he was involved, wanted no parts of it. Eric walked upstairs while Trinoli, Frank and I patiently waited for their arrival.

A few moments later a ring on the doorbell broke our silence. Frank walked to the door and the visitors would press the door bell two more times. "I'm coming," Frank called out. Frank opened the door and two female paramedics stood outside with their ambulance pulled in the driveway. The lights had still been flashing while the sirens were now turned off.

The EMS workers appeared to be in their mid 20's and both were attractive. One had short dirty blonde hair and the other long curly black hair. They seemed to be friendly and quite energetic at this time of night.

"What's problem son?" One of the paramedics asked.

"My friend is unconscious and we can't wake him up." Frank said, answering her question.

The two quickly walked inside and the other said "Where is he?"

"Follow me." Frank said as he turned around and escorted them into the living room as Justin lay on the sofa.

The shorter of the two quickly attended to Justin and checked his pulse and breathing. "What is his name?" She asked.

"Justin." Trinoli answered, as we stood back and watched her examine him.

The other paramedic looked at Frank and said "Why is he all cut up and bleeding? What happened here?"

Frank was given the opportunity to lie or to be straight forward. While we were scared for receiving charges for drinking underage and other offenses Frank decided to tell the truth, or his version of the truth. "Well, we are all graduating in two weeks and I decided to have a little get-together for a few friends. We drank some beer and listened to music and played cards." Frank said as he was stopped by the woman.

"How old are you?" She asked.

"I'll be 18 in a month" Frank answered.

"You know that it is against the law to consume alcohol under the age of 21?" She followed.

"Yes I do." Frank responded.

"Well please continue." She said as the other paramedic began to treat Justin for his cuts.

"Just about everybody left …" Frank said before being interrupted again.

"Who are these two guys?" The paramedic asked, turning around and looking Trinoli and me.

"They are my friends Keith and Mike, They are sleeping here tonight." Frank answered.

"Are your parents aware of this little "Get-Together?" She then asked.

"Yes my Father is aware." Frank said appearing to lose his patience with the woman.

"Are they here?" She asked.

"My Father is out of town for the weekend, he is away for business." Frank said grinding his teeth.

"What about your mother?" She asked continuing her frustrating line of questioning.

"I don't have a mother." Frank said sarcastically.

"Well I am sorry to hear that, could you please continue with your story." She then said.

"Well I am trying to but you keep interrupting me and I am losing my concentration." Frank said. Before giving her the chance for a rebuttal Frank's voice grew louder as he continued.

"Justin came back to my house because he misplaced his cell phone. Once he found it he then left to go home for the night. About 15 minutes or so later he was at my front door cut up and bleeding and said that he was in an accident on Mason Hill road. We tried to keep him awake but he fell asleep. We panicked so I called 911 and now you two lovely ladies are here." Frank said.

The alarming news of the crash had sent the women into frenzy. The paramedic attending the Justin stood up and grabbed her walky talkie that placed on her chest and requested that the police respond an accident on Mason Hill Road. She then looked at her partner and said

"We need to take this boy to the hospital. He does not seem to have any neck trauma or other apparent injury although there is the possibility of internal bleeding and the chance that he has a concussion. His heart beat is normal and he is breathing steadily. I am going to go and get the stretcher."

She ran out of the house to grab the equipment from the ambulance. By now some of Frank's neighbors were peering out their windows to observe the flashing lights.

With her attention now back on Frank the remaining paramedic said "You boy's did the right thing calling us, most people your age don't call 911 because they are afraid of the consequences. But failing to call can sometimes result in death which is truly unfortunate. I want to thank you boys for calling, honestly. You may have saved your friends life tonight."

As her partner returned with a stretcher they carefully placed Justin onto it and began to roll him outside. As they made their way to the door Frank followed and asked "When do you two get off?"

A smile appeared on the woman's face who was speaking with Frank "Although I am flattered that you ask but I don't date younger men, no offense."

"Yeah neither do I, I find them too immature." Frank said.

"You boys have a good night. The police will be here shortly." She said as they hurried outside and loaded Justin into the back of the ambulance. Once he was secure they shut the doors behind them and drove away.

"That wasn't so bad." Trinoli said.

"Yeah, well the cops are still coming." Frank debated "They are the ones we need to worry about."

We waited about 20 minutes and nothing. No one else ever came. We heard no more sirens only the smoke alarm in the kitchen as we had forgotten about the pizza that was cooking in Frank's oven. The Pizza was now burnt to a crisp and ruined, leaving us with nothing to eat.

The police never did show up and we couldn't explain why but we were fortunate none the less. The police did respond to the call regarding the accident and examined the scene. When they observed that no one was hurt and the driver of the crash was taken to the hospital the issue was left it alone for the night. They did, however, note in their records that the cause of the crash was not a result of another car running Justin off of the road as Justin originally told us. There were no skid marks or tire tracks that indicated anything other than that Justin fell asleep at the wheel and drove off of the road.

We anxiously awaited an hour before we tried going to sleep.

Just after 8:15 am the next morning, there was a loud knock at the door followed by the chime of the door bell. Reluctantly Frank stumbled out of bed and headed downstairs to see who could be at his front door so early on the weekend. He opened the door to find an Officer on the other end.

"Good Morning son I'm Officer Tom Pressel. May I come in?" The office asked.

Still tired and disoriented Frank said "Sure."

The officer walked in and took a look around the living room and kitchen. Officer Tom Pressel appeared as if he were on the last leg of duty. Basing by his appearance and stature he had to be close to 60. He was clean shaven except for his old fashioned standard cop mustache. The hair on his face and head were just about completely white. He had dark green eyes that stood out from his older complexion. He was of average height and his uniform was neatly pressed.

"What can I do for you?" Frank asked.

The officer looked at Frank and said "It seems to me like you had a party here last night son. There was a car crash not too far down the road from here, which the driver by the way was here last night consuming alcohol under the age of the 21."

"Yes I know. I called 911 last night. An ambulance came and took him to the hospital. We were waiting all night for you guys to come here but no one ever did." Frank said.

"Well I didn't work last night, and they were never given the proper address. The EMS workers were the first to respond to the call. They do a good job but they tend to forget certain important details from time to time. After the paperwork was filled and the boy was admitted into the hospital we finally got the story straight." The Officer continued. "Now your friend was drinking under the age and endangered his life and was lucky that no one else was on the road. We find underage drinking to be a big offense and don't take these matters lightly son. I know that you called 911 last night and you did the commendable thing and I do respect your honesty."

"Well let me explain officer." Frank interrupted.

"Wait just a minute son and let me finish. Since the incident took place last night and you boys were not administered any kind of a sobriety test we have no evidence of any underage consumption of alcohol and I cannot justifiably charge you with underage drinking. Your friend, however, did receive a concussion from his accident, but it is to my knowledge that he is doing fine. There is a good chance that the reason he is still breathing is because you made the right decision in calling 911. While he wasn't given any alcohol related tests as well, he still smelled of alcohol when the police arrived on scene at the hospital and that just may be enough to warrant a charge of D.U.I and underage drinking." The Officer briefly paused for a second, as he appeared a little out of breathe and then began to cough.

"You'll have to excuse me, my wife thinks all the smoking I do is going to lead to emphysema. I tell her that all her bickering is going to give me a stroke, and I guess at this age I'll take whatever comes first." The Officer said after he regained composure.

"Now, where was I? ... Okay ... It is my intention to let you go with the strictest of warnings son, and only because you were honest and you did the right thing. Honesty is not a quality most people exhibit when speaking to an officer of the law and I find it quite rare when someone of your age tells the truth in these types of circumstances. I have been in this line of business for some 27 odd years. I know a drunk when I see one yet I still pull over these drivers who swear on their mother's grave to me that they are sober." Officer Pressel begins to cough again, pulls out a handkerchief that was neatly folded in his left pants pocket and proceeds to blow his nose.

Officer Pressel refolds the handkerchief and places it back into his pocket and continues. "I have seen far too many young people needlessly die from drinking and driving and other alcohol and drug related accidents that I care for. Many of the times, if not all, these tragedies could easily be avoided. Since you have demonstrated an honorable nature, I am going to give you break."

"Alright" Frank thought to himself as he now realized that he was going to get away Scott free. I remembered a great line from Frank's favorite comedian, George Carlin, "Honesty may be the best policy, but it's important to remember that apparently, by elimination, dishonesty is the second-best policy?" I can even imagine the quote running through his head as the officer informed him he was letting him off the hook.

The irony here was that Frank wasn't always truthful, he lied to everyone. I don't think it was that he was a dishonest person. He just that he enjoyed making others believe his stories. Maybe now Frank would rethink his logic but probably not. That just wasn't Frank.

Officer Pressel cleared his throat and continued "I am going to expect, however, that you perform a minimum of 30 hours of community service. And while I do not have the jurisdiction or authority to administer the community service or enforce that you complete them, if you fail to do so I will be extremely offended and utterly pissed off. Don't take my kindness for a weakness son. For if you and I ever have another encounter and you have disregarded my request, I will make sure that you are prosecuted to the fullest extent of the law. You don't work as a police officer for 27 years and not make any connections and while I may be at the end of my tenure I still have the capacity of making your life hell. Are we clear?"

"Yes officer." Frank answered eagerly.

"Now I am going to give you a sheet with the names and numbers of some local offices that provide services for our community. I am going to periodically check in with them and see if you are keeping up with your end of the bargain." Officer Pressel continued.

"Sounds good to me." Frank said, trying to assure the officer he would follow through on his word thus encouraging him to leave so that he then could go back to sleep.

"As it appears to me your parents are not currently home. I cannot in good conscience leave without explaining to them the situation of our agreement and what has transpired here last night." The officer said, ruining the chances of Frank's father not finding out.

"My Father is away for the weekend on business and won't be back until tomorrow night." Frank said.

"Is there a number that I can reach him at?" Officer Pressel then asked.

"Sure, let know when you're ready." Frank answered before letting out a sigh.

"Let me grab a pen." The officer said as he pulled out a small notebook and a pen. "What's your father's name?"

"Frank McAdams." Frank solemnly replied.

Frank told Officer Pressel his father's cell phone number as he wrote it down in his little notebook. "Well I will give him a call shortly and explain to him what has happened. Remember what I said and stay out of trouble." The officer said.

"I will." Frank replied.

"Enjoy the rest of your day." Officer Pressel said as he adjusted his hat and headed for the front door.

"Yeah you too." Frank said before shutting the door behind the officer. My dad is going to kill me Frank thought, oh well maybe it was worth it.

While no charges were brought against Frank as Officer Pressel promised, Justin, however, was charged with a D.U.I and underage drinking. When Justin appeared in court the Judge dismissed the charges and Justin only faced a misdemeanor and 100 hours of community service.

Later that morning Frank would receive a phone call from an angry father. Needless to say he was quite upset with his son for throwing a party in his absence, and they would discuss Frank's punishment when he got home on Sunday night.

Frank was grounded without use of his cell phone, car and internet for two weeks. The punishment lasted until the night before graduation. Frank said he didn't care too much about his "incarceration." His dad was always at work and worked late nights. I know his father cared for Frank, but it's no wonder Frank acted the way he did. He never had any real guidance or supervision and usually did as he pleased. This was really the first time he was ever reprimanded for his behavior, even with all the stunts he pulled at Arch Bishop Donovan. Frank said he really didn't mind the solitary confinement, he said he just got high and watched a lot of movies, rekindling a love he once had for the silver screen.

# Chapter 26:

It is instinctive to look ahead cautious as to what is awaiting around the corner. If anything I had learned it was to try to enjoy the now. Life isn't a given and we aren't promised tomorrow. Of course it is always easier said than done. I have heard one too many adults tell me that life is too short and to not take our youth granted.

A day that I was feverishly awaiting had now arrived. Tomorrow would mark a new chapter in my life. When you are young and have your whole life in front of you. You walk with vigor in your step and the eagerness in your heart to explore.

I couldn't sleep I was filled with excitement. I jumped out of bed and quickly got dressed. I looked in the mirror and the reflection was daunting. There I stood in graduation attire. The navy blue robe fit flawlessly.

My father was sitting in the living room neatly dressed reading the sports page of newspaper. As he heard me strolling down the hallway he looked up, nodded his head, and began to read the paper again. "Looking good son looking good." He said.

I walked into the kitchen to get a glass of water and there working over the oven was mom. She turned around and instantly had tears in her eyes. "My little boy is all grown up." She said trying to hold back emotions. She walked closer as she examined the cap and gown. She threw her arms around me, kissed my check twice and said "You look so handsome, why don't you have a girlfriend?"

"Oh, stop it Mom." I said trying to hide a subtle smile. "Please don't embarrass me today, okay?"

"How could your mother, who loves you, ever embarrass you?" Mom asked.

"I'm sure you could find a way." I said jokingly. "Anyway, what's cooking good looking?"

Mom was an artist in the kitchen. The family didn't normally eat breakfast together, only on holidays and special occasions. We did, however, regularly have dinner promptly at 5:30 and if you weren't in your seat when after the dinner bell rang there was hell to pay. The dinner table was the source of some memorable conversation. As much as I complained that I had to be home for dinner at a certain time for dinner, I always had a bigger gripe when mom didn't feel like cooking. Having our family dinners were a staple of my childhood.

The commencement ceremony was scheduled for 10 am. All graduating seniors were to be at the high school promptly at 8:15. Teachers were stationed to monitor attendance and ensure that graduates were in their proper location. The stage was set out on the football field we would receive our diplomas and toss our hats. Just fewer than 600 students would be celebrating on this morning, June 2nd 2001. It was a long way from the 1,100 who first started the journey. Almost 100 hundred failed to reach commencement day in their senior year.

I arrived to my designated homeroom and filled out some paperwork. I watched as additional sashes were given to honor students and although I did not receive one I realized that I should have. During our graduation practices we were given assigned seating that was based by last name. A few friends and I had discussed switching seating arrangements and congregating in the back so that we could share our final moments as high school students together.

Time is an unusually phenomena. Time seems to never be in accordance to what one expects or desires. Time has the uncanny ability to quickly change speed and it seems to me that there are only two settings: extremely slow and dauntingly fast. Rarely do we compliment Time for its consistent steady approach. Never compromising but always on time.

The twelve years of formal education leading to this moment had felt like an eternity. A life time of waiting to be able to enter adulthood was here. As a child all I really wanted was freedom. And now it seems that every adult wishes to not be burdened with the responsibility that freedom brings. Now I was going to find if this was really what I wanted.

We were lead out onto the football field. It was a beautiful day you could count the number of clouds on two fingers. The seats were neatly arranged leaving a wide path for the center aisle. The stands were filled with excited parents with cameras in one hand and graduation programs in the other. A roar of excitement echoed when all the mothers and fathers saw their graduates take center stage. Just as we promised we took the last two rows on the right hand side.

Principal Cald quickly arose and stepped to the podium. "Congratulations Seniors, you did it, your journey is now complete. As you sit here before me you are now high school graduates. Your lives are ahead of you. You are now entering an unfamiliar world, a world in which you are not quite fully prepared, for no one can ever truly be prepared for the unexpected, but now you have the education and experience to help guide you. What you have learned here at John Adams are stepping stones to your future. Use what you have learned here to your fullest advantage. While you are responsible for your future, I encourage you to go after your dreams. If you do not know what it is you are looking for, give yourself the opportunity to succeed. I see a lot of promise in this year's graduating class and you should be proud of your accomplishments today. Life is a journey which begins with one single step. No step shall be overlooked for our path cannot be completed without it. One that note I will leave you with this: Life is an ever evolving chess match. In order to succeed one must use strategy and well thought decisions to advance to the next step and yet one wrong move can result in dire consequence. We start out as pawns making small moves toward our goal in hopes to one day to be the king. "

The rest of the ceremony was a really blur. Speaker after speaker stepped to the podium and read their notes and delivered their motivational words of encouragement and a positive outlook of our next steps. To me, a graduation ceremony is really a formality. A reason for teachers and administration to get dressed up in their gowns so they too can be praised on the work they have done by educating and graduating their students. Call me cynical if you will, but they could have just given me a diploma and it would have been all the same. Parents are the one who seem to care the most I guess.

The final speech was given by the senior class president Megan Douglas. Ms. Douglas decided to entertain the audience with tears of joy and emotion as she spoke of our last four years at John Adams High School

The tradition of changing the side of the tassel and then tossing the graduation caps high into the air was well executed as the crowd furiously snapped their cameras. It was official. We were free. Never look back they say, always look ahead.

We had met up with our families while we were bombarded with the phrase "Say Cheese!"As the group smiled I thought to myself, what now?

# Chapter 27:

If there is a fine line between genius and insanity and right from wrong, how fine of a line defines our perception of reality? It takes time to learn how to decipher false from truth. In order to perceive what is reality does one need to know what they are looking for.

I found in life that one must be able to adapt or prepare to be forgotten. It took quite some time to adjust to this current philosophy despite sound advice. Some lessons can only be learned through personal experience.

If adversity is a true test of one's character, life will undoubtedly present us a lot of exams and a shortage of number two pencils. Just when you think you've got it down, the rules change.

Next year I would start all over again. I would Montgomery University in the fall of 200, another milestone to reach. Montgomery University was just over 60 miles north of my home in the city. I was looking forward to the change in atmosphere and scenery. My father and I had visited the communications department and sat in on a class and observed. The size of the class was a little different than what I had expected. There were at least 125 students enrolled in the course. I would enter Montgomery University majoring in Communication Studies. I fell in love with the communications course that I was enrolled in m senior year at John Adams and it was my intention to continue studying it.

The night before I would leave for college my father sat me down and said to me "There isn't anything in this world that you can't do if you put your mind to it son, just remember to always dream like a young man, with the wisdom of an old man. We have big dreams when we are young and then there comes a time when reality sets in. Never let anything discourage you from you want, the only thing that can hold you back in this life is yourself. You are capable of anything you set your mind too." My father then handed me a gold bicentennial pocket watch that my mother gave to him as an anniversary present in 1976. As he gave me the watch with tear filled eyes he said "I've been waiting to give you this you're whole life."

I would stay close with a number of friends I had made at John Adams. Trinoli and Eric would also attend Montgomery University in the fall. Trinoli would make the Universities football team as a cornerback. After 5 games he quit due to the coaches intolerable demeanor. Later Trinoli would join the school's Rugby team. We would stay friends throughout college. Before graduating he would spend a semester in Rome and developed a taste for the finer things in life. After graduating he took an extremely lucrative sales position in Miami Florida through a connection he had made in Europe. I have since visited him twice.

Eric would become an honor student and frequently made the dean's list during his tenure at Montgomery University. We would live in the same dorm our freshman year and I tried to convince him to pledge a fraternity with me during the spring semester. After thorough consideration he felt that it wasn't for him. Our friendship would flutter as we would head in separate directions. In our sophomore year during Christmas break he would fall in love with a girl from back home and would eventually transfer to schools so that they could be closer. They are still together and recently were engaged. Last time we spoke he was hired as a web designer for an up and coming internet company Google.

Bobby Jackson never did play football in the collegiate level. Maryland University rescinded their offer and scholarship after his injury. After visiting a number of specialists, many doctors told him that his injury was the worst foot injury they had ever seen. They told Bobby that he would have been better off if the bone fractured. The injury never truly healed and too this day he still walks with a noticeable limp. Bobby tried to get other schools to let him try out for their teams but they just didn't want to take a chance on the former All American Linebacker. Bobby eventually got into a community college for two years and was later accepted to Temple University. Bobby would receive a teaching degree and with a focus in coaching and was hired by John Adams High school as a gym teacher. He became an assistant coach for the football team with the hopes of one day being a defensive coordinator at the university level. His commitment to never give up is inspiring.

Principal Cald's act of charity to allow the admission of expelled transfer students would almost immediately result in regret. A few months in the 2002 school year at John Adams High school a number of students who benefited from the program were cutting class and were right outside of the cafeteria. They students formed a large circle and participated in what was called a "Beat Battle." Those involved competed by trying to "out rap" their opponent. An unwary freshman unsuspectingly broke through the circle on his way to the bathroom. Enraged by the boy's act of disrespect he was beaten to within an inch of his life. The hood of his sweatshirt was pulled down over his head after being thrown to the ground. The boy was repeatedly kicked in the head. After being rushed to the hospital the boy was diagnosed with brain damage. While the student would recover from his other wounds he would never again be the same. His attackers fled the scene and were never caught. All that was offered was the testimonials from a few eye witnesses who refused to come to the victim's aide for fear or their own safety.

Principal Cald retired a month after the preliminary medical evaluation of the now handicapped student as the event weighed heavily on his conscience. He claimed that the past few years had cause mounting stress and mental fatigue. He said that it was just his time to go off to pasture and pursue other things.

Principal Cald's passion for mentoring and guiding young men and women had come to an end. Like I said before it's hard to educate those who do not wish to be educated. It is even harder to facilitate them. The school system was more concerned with truancy and unfortunately for Principal Cald and Adams High too many students seemed unfit to teach.

My mother now grew increasingly worried about the learning environment of her youngest son and against Derek's will she made the decision that Derek would be transferred out of Adams High. Her intentions were that Derek could finish his final two years in a sound institution where his mind would be focused on his studies and not school security. Derek was transferred to a nearby co-ed catholic school.

As a part of school curriculum Derek would take a mandatory S.A.T. prep class. Derek graduated with high honors and was accepted to Penn State University for the fall semester of 2003. I never was envious that he achieved what I did not. I was proud of his accomplishments. He took advantage of the opportunity to not commit the same mistakes I had made. As fate would have it Wendi Miller was accepted to play field hockey at Penn State University and they began dating at the end of Derek's freshman year. They broke up a year later. Currently Derek is at the University of Pittsburgh getting his masters degree in Psychology. He wants to be a teacher.

As for Frank, well, Frank never technically graduated. He just so happened to forget to tell his father, and the rest of us for that matter, that he was failing math and science. He would have to receive his GED during the summer. Franks father thought he lacked the discipline and responsibility that was necessary to one day take over the family business. Franks father gave him the ultimatum of joining the military or too move out and get a real job. Frank enlisted in the Army and was set to leave for boot camp at the end of the summer of 2001. Frank was able to convince his recruiter to let him start his "sentence," a little earlier and left for boot camp three days after the 4th of July.

During my freshman year of college I was walking back to my dorm from an early morning class when a friend of mine informed me that two planes crashed into one another in New York City. That's odd I thought to myself. A few moments later my mom called my phone. "We're being attacked" she screamed. "We're being attacked by Terrorists, turn on the TV!"

The unthinkable was unfolding on Television as the United States was attacked by a terroristic assault as four commercial airliners were hijacked by members of Al-Qaeda. Two of the four planes were intentionally crashed into the Twin Towers of the World Trade Center. The buildings collapsed within two hours and caused panic and devastation as the fall of the World Trade Center destroyed other buildings and killing many innocent American men and women. A third plane was crashed into the Pentagon and the fourth fell to ground in a rural part of Pennsylvania after passengers attempted to regain control of the hijacked plane. 2,973 people died that day. It was the most significant attack on American soil.

After 9/11 Frank was be deployed to fight in Afghanistan and then stationed in Iraq. He once wrote me a letter describing what it was like, and that he really didn't mind it there. He wrote "the Army thinks I'm responsible enough to carry a loaded assault rifle, I'm happy."

On a Tuesday afternoon my sophomore year in college I got a phone call from Mom. She called to inform that Frank McAdams was killed by a car bomb right outside of Bagdad. He and two other soldiers were driving into town when a suicide bomber ran over to their vehicle and detonated a bomb that was strapped to his chest. Later that night the news was on NBC's news broadcast. They had a picture of all three soldiers. My heart sank from chest.

Frank's father could never forgive himself for forcing his son into the military and held himself responsible for Frank's death. He sold his business and quietly left the area.

A part of me never really got over Frank's death. It was the first time in my life someone close to me died. Franks father had decided to have a small ceremony for immediate family. I never really got the chance to say goodbye. I often think back to the fun we had and the outrageous stories he told. He was a good person and a great friend. I never really told Frank what his relationship had meant to me. Some words are never intended to be spoken. The message has already been. The last time I saw Frank was the night before he had left for boot camp. I can only begin to imagine all the stunts he pulled in the Army. Those stories were left untold.

He made one trip home for a weekend before being shipped off to Iraq. He didn't come up and visit me at college because he didn't want to upset his father. He asked me to come home but I was selfish and didn't go home. I couldn't get a ride from my parents and was too lazy to take the train. The decision still haunts me. I never cried after Frank's death, not until I read his father's memorial invitation letter some 9 years later.

# Chapter 28:

Mr. Harrison once said that "Where you start is not as important as where you finish, and that you get to the finish line through hard work and dedication"

I was never one to believe that things happen for a reason. I do not think that our lives our predetermined, but I am finding out that things have a peculiar way of unfolding. Sometimes unforeseen events cannot be explained.

Through my parents and education I was handed the tools and resources necessary for success and proper development, it was my decisions that decided the outcome. Over the course of my short life unexpected events occurred for with I was unprepared. Life teaches you to learn, grow and adapt.

For every moment, you have one opportunity to get it right. Life does not come with a reset button. I often imagine if I could revisit past failures and improve their outcome, but learning the value of their lessons will have to do. My father always said the key to success is from learning from our mistakes and not repeating them.

I always wanted to be perfect, but if you really think about it, perfection can be an ugly word. Not one single person, event or thing is or ever will be perfect. Perfection can create false identities and unobtainable realities. I will always strive to be my best, but I am only human.

As I sit on the couch with both Invitations in my hand still reminiscent of the past I notice that both invitations are scheduled on the same Saturday night. That's what I call irony. Without hesitation of further thought my mind is made up. I stand up from the couch and walk into the kitchen. I open then cabinet door underneath the sink and toss out one of the invitations into the trash. I place the remaining invitation on the counter as I search for a magnet on the refrigerator door. It's always so cluttered from all the coupons and miscellaneous items my girlfriend likes save. I make some room on door and hang the letter from the magnetic paper clip.

I walk over to the Calendar flip a few months and circle Saturday October 14th to remind myself of the memorial dinner. I never got to say good bye to you Frank and now I will get that chance.

My cell phone rings. It's my girlfriend is calling.

"Hey babe, whets up?" I say as I answer the phone.

"Where have you been? I've called you like three times." She asks sounding impatient.

"I've been here at the apartment. I didn't see that you called." I reply.

"We'll I was running late from work. Did you want to meet me at Chili's for dinner?" She asks.

"Sure. Meet you there in 5 minutes?" I said as I grabbed my keys and headed for the door.

"I'll see you then, bye I love you." She says.

"I love you too." I say back.

"Wait...Did we get any mail?" She gets in before I can hang up.

"Yes we did. I'll tell you about it when I get there." I say.